I0761398

The World Between

Also by Zeeva Bukai

The Anatomy of Exile

The

World Between

a novel

Zeeva Bukai

Delphinium Books

THE WORLD BETWEEN

Printed in the United States of America

For information, address DELPHINIUM BOOKS
1250 4th Street, 5th Floor
Santa Monica, California 90401

Library of Congress Catalog-in-Publication Data is available on request.
ISBN 978-1-953002-67-9

Jacket and interior design by Colin Dockrill, AIGA

In memory of my mother, Rosa,

and grandmother, Cyla.

1.

My dear, by now Rothman has given you the news in his usual officious manner that I am under observation at the Sisters of Saint Joseph of the Apparition Hospice in Jaffa while this misunderstanding is being investigated. I hope he hasn't implied that I've been arrested or given the impression that I am incapacitated, or God forbid, that you need to leave the comforts of our apartment in New York for Tel Aviv now that you've been apprised of the situation. Please, *liebchen*, don't even consider it. You know how Rothman exaggerates. Besides, he has no idea how much you detest flying or how unsettled you get venturing out of our Upper West Side neighborhood. Nor does he know how attached you are to Stein's newsstand on Broadway and 92nd Street, the only place on the West Side that still sells *The Folksbiene Gazette* along with those violet candies you like. And what about

Zabar's? I've never seen white fish salad or corned beef in any of the local shops or markets here. God knows there isn't a bagel to be had, not the kind you're used to. No, it's best you stay home. And please don't pay any attention to what Rothman says because I have not, as he so eloquently put it, lost my marbles. At least the doctor treating me doesn't think so. Dr. S is a well-respected physician in this institution. He has charged me to write this letter as part of what he calls my wellness plan.

Corral your thoughts, he says, and then after a great puff on his meerschaum pipe, he points a fatherly finger at me and advises, Tell your husband everything. He'll understand.

Dr. S often speaks in declarative sentences as a way to spur his patients to action. I admit, my mind whips here and there, summoning up all manner of debris. But Dr. S insists that I get the facts down on paper and state unequivocally that I am well attended to here. I will regain my strength and return home to you. Our lives will resume their natural course. Which is to say, I will be myself again very soon.

2.

It was decent of Rothman to bring me an extra blanket and down pillow. You'll be happy to know that I am as comfortable as one can be away from their own bed. The hospice is small and modest, run by a group of French nuns, built in 1827 as a respite for weary pilgrims on their way to Jerusalem. I can see them disembarking from a ship named the *Belle Nazarene* at the Jaffa port. Fierce sunlight bleaching the stones of the old city, blinding the passengers as porters in white kaffiyehs and djellabas stack their portmanteaus on donkey carts. Whenever I look at the garden, I imagine those God-fearing folk who traveled more than a thousand miles by sea to reach the holy land, sitting in the shade of a banyan tree, nibbling on brioche and oranges before their journey to the sacred city, where they will walk through the Via Dolorosa in the footsteps of Jesus, then march outside the gates to Golgotha and stand in the place where he was crucified.

The Sisters wear black floor-length habits and veils that smell of lilacs and ammonia cleaner. Framed in wimples, they look like daisies, but when they're in the dim corridors, their heads appear to float off their necks. They rarely smile, and when they speak, it's often in a reverent whisper, as though God is walking alongside them, listening to their every word. I have to lean in to hear them or ask them to repeat themselves, which annoys them, I think, though they don't show it except in the slight pursing of their lips. Still, Rothman was right to insist on bringing me here instead of one of the big, modern hospitals where I might have been recognized. The hospice is more like a sanitarium, a European spa our parents might have frequented before the war. We're close enough to the sea so that at dawn when I lie in my narrow bed, I can hear the waves break along the fortress wall and the fishing boats bob against the docks. Some mornings I can even smell the fishermen's haul, their nets full of St Peter's fish and shrimp, the air tangy with salt.

There is a school next door, the *Collège des Frères*. From my window I can see the statue of Saint Joseph perched like a guardian angel on the roof of their building. I like to peek into the courtyard below, where the boys have their morning recess. They play baseball, much like the children in Riverside Park do on Saturday and Sunday afternoons. I listen for when the bat strikes the ball. If the angle is right, there's a resounding crack like the sound of a car that's backfired. Crows burst from the Aleppo pines, and for a moment they are a Rorschach inkblot come to life.

The boys are so young, Max. At the end of recess, they charge to the stone fountain in the center of the courtyard and wash their hands and feet before returning to the classroom. It's a wondrous sight, those boys tearing off their shoes and socks with such abandon, their feet slender as fish, splashing and cavorting. When they leave, the courtyard retracts into silence, and between beams of sunlight, shadows bloom. A monk in brown robes patrols the grounds, searching for laggards and strays behind the Ionic columns. When he finds one, he lifts him up by the ear and drags the child back inside. I have to clamp a hand over my mouth to stop myself from shouting at him to let the boy go.

Did I mention this room was once a nun's cell? There's a picture of Jesus on the wall. He gazes up at heaven as if to say, *Is this really what you had in mind?* At first, I found his presence in the room impossible. It's enough that on every wall and in every corner of the hospice there are crucifixes and large paintings of him. In some he is blond; in others he is brunette. In all, he's half naked, beset by nails and thorns, the agony and ecstasy of his sacrifice and martyrdom on full display. He hovers between life and death, and the confluence of these driving forces results in an almost unbearable intimacy. I try to explain this to Dr. S and ask, Am I expected to live with this all-suffering man-god in my room?

Learn to accept where you are, he admonishes, and stop dwelling on things you cannot change.

I took down the picture of Jesus. A few hours later the nuns found him in my closet and nailed him to the wall. I've kept him there ever since. What choice do I have? Now he is my companion in all things. Each morning I bare my ancient body to him, and he kindly pretends not to notice the decrepitude.

3.

Rothman tells me you're worried my condition may be permanent. Be assured I suffer only from a slight nervous exhaustion. No more than a bad case of jet lag. You know what a poor sleeper I am, even in the best of circumstances. Remember the hotel we stayed in during our performance of Ansky's play in Los Angeles? I couldn't fall asleep there either, no matter how comfortable the beds were. And there was that business with the young woman, you know the one I mean, Miss Polka Dots, who came backstage every night insisting you had invited her there. How you looked at me, your face red as a schoolboy's caught with his fly open. I don't know how I got through the run of the play. The window in our hotel room didn't open, and all I could see was the parking lot. Not even a shrub to relieve the eye. In the distance, smoke rose from out of the hills like they were sacrificing goats up there. At night when we returned from the theater and you fell into bed exhausted, I stayed awake listening to a child cry in the next room, calling to her mother. All night long she keened Mama, Mama, finally stopping just as the sun rose over the brown hills.

I promise you there is no need for concern. So, I get the occasional headache. That's all it is. Though sometimes there is a sharp pain that travels from the hinge of my jaw to the back of my neck, but I'm sure there is a simple explanation for it. As for the underwater trapped-like-Houdini feeling, well, you more than anyone know how sensitive I am. Honestly, there's nothing to worry about. The sensation that I straddle two worlds—the world of nothing and the world of everything—and that I am *nischt ahin, nischt aher*, neither here nor there, will soon pass. Besides, it isn't the first time my mind wades into the past like a fish that has slipped its net.

Did you ask Rothman to take a photograph of me holding up the front page of the newspaper like some nebach who's been kidnapped? Really

Max, it's demoralizing and unfair. All right, so it's difficult for me to determine what day it is, but I know it's March because the cyclamen are in bloom, and I know it's 1998 because I left New York in December. The Sisters deliberately keep that information from us. There are no calendars. We do not see a newspaper. The radio is never on, though I often hear someone playing the piano in the sunroom. The same piece again and again. The entire facility is infused with this music. A Chopin nocturne, I think, though I could be wrong. A Chopin nocturne haunts us.

4.

Today Dr. S addressed a peculiar sensation that I've been having—that time is suspended here.

The confusion between reality and memory is to be expected, he says, and will pass once I'm fully rested and am released from this place. But, Max, I'm unconvinced. He hasn't said when I'll be discharged. It may be as soon as tomorrow, but I have no idea to which tomorrow he refers. There's an eternity of tomorrows here. Be so kind as to ask him when I can leave. I'm sure he'll listen to you, especially if you tell him I'm needed at home. Let's forget the other business, shall we? And think only of what we've been and meant to each other all these years.

I must go. The orderly has arrived with my medication. I know how you hate it when I take even an aspirin, but please don't fret. It's only a mild sedative. I hope he's brought the carrot juice I requested. They make it fresh here. *Bis morgen, liebchen.*

5.

Oh my dear, I should have never mentioned your play *Di Bloy Dame* to Dr. S. He pounced on the information like a lion on a zebra and grilled me for over an hour. Unfortunately, I let slip that it was the first time I detested a character you wrote. Truly, the very first time. We spent most of the session dissecting the Blue Lady's hunger for power. Not an ounce of motherly love in her except at the end when she learns the child who has died is her own. All this time I've wondered why you'd create such a detestable character and thought maybe it was my fault for dragging the past out into the open so often, though it could easily have been one of your female students trying to tear the scabs off your war wounds, believing only she could heal you, not knowing that you didn't want to be healed.

6.

This morning Dr. S asked, How would you categorize your marriage?

What do you mean? I said.

What image comes to mind?

An iceberg, I quipped.

We were in his office. It was one of those spring days when the sun drenched the room in an almost holy light.

He leaned his elbows on the desk and steepled his fingers. You've been married forty years or so.

That's right.

It couldn't all have been icy.

No. The opposite, in fact, I said.

He waited for me to continue. I turned my face toward the window, where the sun beamed, and behind shuttered eyes a red desert appeared like a mirage, stark and wavering as if the landscape were on fire.

* * *

I remember you were standing outside the theater, signing autographs for the few fans who'd gathered near the stage entrance. It must have been in the fall of '78. We'd been in the States for twenty years by then. You wore your fedora cocked at a rakish angle and a black cape draped over your shoulders like some nineteenth-century impresario. You were so handsome. Your blue eyes gleaming. And I beside you, smiling, always smiling, especially when our friends visited on Sundays after a matinee at one of the derelict theaters on the old Jewish Rialto on the Lower East Side, palaces haunted by the glories of the past. I filled plates with canapés and shot glasses with schnapps. The herring floated in bowls of sour cream and onions, and the pumpernickel and rye were stacked on a gleaming silver tray. The arguments spilled into laughter. I made sure the music was right, a bit of Liszt for the older crowd. Jobim for your students who dropped in for a drink and free meal. The hungry young women you seemed to attract, slipping off their coats and loafers, acolytes at your feet, smoking unfiltered Turkish cigarettes, drinking our liquor and practicing their Yiddish, a dead language in the house of a terminal marriage.

I made sure the ashtrays were emptied, filled the

ice bucket, and enjoyed watching you hold court, lapping the attention you garnered whenever there was a crowd. Deflating after they'd leave. You'd ask if it was all worth it and I'd rub your shoulders and say, Of course, *meine leibe*, and tell you what an important man you were, how much you were revered and loved. The last Yiddish playwright in New York desperate to hold on to a world that no longer existed, perhaps had never existed except in your imaginative longing to recreate the world your parents inhabited, as if by doing so, you could resurrect them. Perhaps you thought you could resurrect us. I wanted to think so.

Sometimes you said the most outrageous things just to get a rise out of our friends. There was one conversation with a particularly beautiful actress, smart in her red silk dress and black suede pumps. You told her there was no difference between an actor and a wooden dummy. Everyone stopped to listen. I was at the edge of the living room, holding a tray of dirty glasses, and I winced. I saw you, a man who thrived on attention. You needed it to confirm proof of life, proof that you were worthy enough to have survived the war, and that you still mattered.

And what does that make you, she said, tilting her head back so that the tendons in her neck stretched taut, revealing the soft pulse of a ropey blue vein.

A ventriloquist, you said.

Someone turned off the phonograph. The tension in the room was palpable.

She drew very close, her body brushing against yours. One or two women sent me pitying glances, but I knew better. She wasn't your type, a bit too overblown and eager, a fraction too old. She had a cynicism about her that put you off, and most of all, she was independent. She didn't need you. She didn't even rely on you for a good role.

Oh, the actress said with just the right amount of pout to her lips.

You caught my gaze and winked. My stomach knotted.

I'm the ventriloquist who plants words in your mouth except maybe when you're . . . , and then you leaned down and whispered in her ear and she blushed. Everyone laughed. They could all guess what racy thing you said, yet I had a sickening feeling that what you uttered in her ear was not only vulgar but brutal. At the time I needed to believe you were just having a bit of fun, that you didn't actually see yourself as the man who pulled the strings. But two decades later, I couldn't delude myself any longer, not after the rehearsals for *Di Bloy Dame*. I realized then how much you had changed, how the dynamics in our relationship had undergone a paradigm shift, and I knew that you had meant every word.

7.

In our next session, Dr. S asked me to consider not just why you wrote *Di Bloy Dame*, but when you wrote it.

Two years ago, I said, startled to realize that you began writing the play around the time Rothman's third wife gave birth to a baby girl. This unsettled you, and I asked if you wished you'd had a young wife.

Hidden behind the *Gazette*, you practically growled, Don't be an idiot. What the hell would I do with another wife? Tell me, you said, tossing the paper aside, why does that bastard get a second chance? Why does he always get everything?

I don't know, I said, but I understood something that day. Your anger or jealousy or anguish, whatever it was, had to do with the child, not Rothman.

* * *

None of that really matters now but it's important that you know I didn't want to hate your play. God forgive me, I just couldn't find anything redeeming in it, not the characters, the plot, definitely not the indigo set, or the blue costumes and elaborate wigs I was forced to wear. You even had the makeup artist tint my skin. The critics thought it made me look like I'd died of hypothermia. And during tech week in front of cast and crew you shouted, *Why, can't you fucking get her right?* In the forty-five years we've lived together, worked together, you've never raised your voice at me in the theater, our one true temple. Opening night, you waited in the wings, and when I stepped offstage for a costume change, you pinched my arm and hissed:

Stop trying to get the audience's sympathy.

You'd think it would be a relief to drown that woman in a bath of indigo dye each night, only it wasn't, Max. I was the one drowning. Even Dr. S agrees that destroying her destroyed us a little.

Last spring, I shut myself up for weeks after the show closed and didn't come out until Rothman's visit. He dragged me to Riverside Park while the Polish nanny took care of the new daughter and wife number three was downtown buying out half of Loehmann's.

You look like *dreck*, Rothman said, and fed me cinnamon rugelach from Orwashers Bakery and, to wash it down, a flask of peach schnapps. I didn't feel like talking, so we watched in silence as the boats sailed on the river. I don't know where you were that day, meeting with your students on campus or at the theater on the Lower East Side or maybe you were at the Carlyle across town, where you liked to reserve a room. A place of your own to write, to conduct business, to rendezvous with some nubile freshman who stopped you from feeling like your time was running out. A few hours to give you the freedom you thought you wanted. Rothman read to me a three-month-old review in the *Forward* that he kept in his wallet. They said my performance in *Di Bloy Dame* was electrifying, "a high wire act of shattering realism." They thought you were brilliant. For five minutes we were the darlings of the Yiddish theater, which is really quite something, considering it's been dead for seventy years. All we'd been doing for decades was keeping the corpse warm.

I told Dr. S that I am no longer angry with you for insisting I play her, for torturing me with your rages and silences, your banging of pots and pans at all hours and prowling around the apartment, gnawing at your fingernails until I agreed to do the part. I owed it to you, you said. My punishment for past sins, though you hadn't yet revealed to me what they were. Dr. S believes me, but you know me better, Max. I forget nothing.

You have to admit that *Di Bloy Dame* was a departure from your other plays, none of which were successful in Broadway terms but at least they had heart. I still love the modest butchers, the nimble tailors, the fat grocers with their *geshefts* and nagging wives who die of longing and consumption. The daughters who fall in love with the traveling merchant. The demon that steals in at night through a pinhole of lost faith. I don't think you understand what you accomplished with your plays. You married innocence with the demonic, the lovelorn with the cynical. You made the old world live inside the new. You made it live inside us and helped recover what was lost. How many successful Hebrew-Yiddish playwrights are there in New York City? For that matter, how many Hebrew-Yiddish actresses are there?

B'emes, I wish you'd never written *Di Bloy Dame*. We'd have been better off without her.

Dr. S suggests I meditate on my anger.

Zeeva Bukai

Rage serves only to obfuscate neurosis, he says.
But it's ever so clean, I reply.

8.

I've finally met the pianist. That ghost. The one who haunts us with his arpeggios and whatnot. After lunch, Sister Francoise escorted me to the sunroom. He was dressed in a pair of brown-and-white-striped pajamas with a matching silk robe. *Nebach.* He wore leather slippers on his feet. The kind my papa kept parked by his bedside. The man is at least ten years older than I am, but on the piano bench he sits like a king on a throne. Thick white hair sweeps off a high, protruding forehead. All that cranium showing, all of it stuffed with Chopin nocturnes.

The regulars in the sunroom, a man and a woman about my age, sixty or seventy, in a state of disarray—not because of any negligence on the part of the staff. They start off neatly dressed in the morning, faces washed, hair combed. It's the clothes they can't abide. They're always tugging at them, so that by the afternoon the clothes are as misshapen as burlap sacks. They bumble around the sunroom and plant themselves near the French doors that lead to the garden. The two of them gaze at the banyan tree as though the answer to what's befallen them is hidden beneath the curtain of aerial roots, a riddle they can't solve.

The pianist had a new audience today. Rothman and his eldest daughter, Pnina, decided to surprise me. Poor girl looked ready to bolt. I could have shot Rothman for dragging her here. What was he trying to do, scare her? Had he warned me, I'd have put on a good dress, washed my hair, worn a bit of lipstick instead of looking so *shvach*. Rothman's seen me at my worst, but his daughter was shocked by what he's snidely come to refer to as my metamorphosis from glorious butterfly to lowly caterpillar. She's too polite to say anything, but I could tell by the way her eyes searched for the exit that I looked exactly like what I am, what I always was and will be—a refugee, a prisoner of war, a woman trapped inside her skull.

Pnina is all grown up. A beautiful girl. Rothman says there's a young man, but now that she's graduated Hebrew University with a degree in industrial design, she wants to be like her father, an impresario, a patron of the arts. She has no idea how Rothman makes his millions—the wheeling and dealing in back rooms with shady politicians and Panamanian businessmen. A little import here, export there, a bit of grease to make customs officials look the other way when a shipment arrives from Sri Lanka or Malawi and all the while the shekels pour into Rothman's pockets. He'll let her handle a concert or two and then marry her off to the young American lawyer he's picked out for her.

The pianist hadn't even begun before Rothman and Pnina jumped to their feet.

I'm having a dinner party in a few weeks, you should come, Pnina said and kissed my cheek. That producer, what's his name, Dudu Epstein? The one who worked on *Di Bloy Dame* will be there, and Max said he'd try to make it too. I wish I could have seen you in that play. Aba said you were magnificent.

I smiled, I think, or tried to. Meanwhile, Sister Francoise, ever alert, noticed how pale I'd become and asked if I wanted to return to my room.

No, thank you, I said.

Sister Francoise appreciates politeness above

all else and says it fosters good relations, and if everyone made a point of being polite, there would be no conflict and no war. Of course, if you're impolite, Sister Francoise doesn't hesitate to let you know with a biting remark and a swift *flick* on the wrist.

The pianist, I'll call him Tomasz for a boy I once knew who had drowned in a lake in Krosniewice not far from where my parents lived and where Rothman and his eldest sister were our neighbors. Tomasz was my childhood friend, and my happiest days were when he and Rothman let me tag along on one of their adventures. I don't know why he's surfaced in my thoughts now, except there's something about the pianist, a tender, faraway look that comes over him when he plays that reminds me of Tomasz tossing stones into the lake where he met his end. He was a delicate boy, maybe eleven or twelve, slender with thick auburn hair. It was spring and the snow melt caused the water to rise. The current, like a pair of arms, gathered him up and whirled him away. His father found him the next morning trapped in the reeds on the northern bank, staring wide-eyed at the sky. Rothman and I were inconsolable. We spent most of that spring and summer at the lake waiting, it seemed, for

Tomasz to return from wherever it is that the dead go. And then in September the war broke out. I don't know what happened to Tomasz's family, whether they stayed in Krosniewice or, like us, fled to the east of Poland before the Germans invaded. We had no way of knowing that we would be stuck there or that the Soviets would deport us to Siberia and that it would be years before we'd return. When we finally did in '46, we learned no one we knew had survived. We found shelter in a barn two kilometers from what was left of the Jewish cemetery.

It's hard being here, Rothman said.

I agreed, thinking he meant without our families and with nowhere to stay.

But then he said Tomasz's name. His breath ragged; the words scraped up from some deep abandoned well.

I loved him, he said.

More than me? I said, and felt a pinch in my heart.

He squeezed my hand. You're family.

And Tomasz?

Rothman looked up at the splinters of light flooding the cracks in the slatted walls. His expression vacant, lost.

He was my friend, he said.

I lay my head in his lap and felt his loneliness seep under my skin.

It may seem strange to you, Max, but knowing how much Rothman loved him made me love Tomasz even more. In death, he became the conduit to Rothman's heart. I can still see the three of us lying in the tall grasses on the southern bank of the lake where no one ventured. And once when they didn't know that I had followed them, I saw them strip out of their clothes and plunge into the deep end of the stream in the forest where we were warned not to go. Rothman was trying to teach him to swim. He leaned down to whisper something in his ear and Tomasz pressed his face into Rothman's neck. Their boyish beauty, their intimacy, an ache I couldn't reconcile.

They stayed like that for a long while, Tomasz cradled in Rothman's arms, the water undulating around them, the forest of black alder trees throbbing with life.

The pianist cracked his knuckles. Sister Francoise stood in a shaft of light. Her long, thin face the image of a medieval saint. I was half paralyzed. Rothman understood immediately and asked

Pnina to wait for him outside.

Did I do something wrong? she asked, anxiously looking from me to her father.

No, no, I patted her hand. The pills they give me make me a little dizzy, that's all, I said.

When she left, I turned to Rothman, heart in my mouth, and asked if you were coming here.

But he shook his head and, without Sister Francoise noticing, slipped a hundred-shekel note into my hand.

For God's sake, get some makeup and hair dye, he said, and then with a gentle smile continued, You look like hell, and kissed my cheek.

After Rothman left, I stayed to listen to Tomasz play the nocturne, each mournful note swelling into the ward.

Please understand, it's not that I don't want you here, Max. It's just that I'm not at my best yet and I know how difficult it would be for you to see me this way, no matter the circumstances between us. You aspire to perfection in all things. I'm not complaining, my dear. It's an admirable trait, and I'm sure I'll be my old self again very soon. Not a hair out of place, manicured, flawless makeup, the right jewels with the right bag, the right shoes with the right dress. A perfect size six. You see, I haven't forgotten how you once loved me best.

9.

I told Rothman he was a thoughtless lout for bringing Pnina here. He knew I wasn't ready for visitors. There was a half-hearted apology, which of course I accepted. Staying angry at Rothman is like staying angry at myself. What good will it do? He'll only come back with something unexpected, something I cannot resist like a bottle of passionflower liqueur imported from France, which costs a fortune here, or an apple cake the Polish nanny baked, or a beloved book I'd lost years ago and mentioned one day in passing, a book no longer in print and my distress at its loss fresh as if it had disappeared that morning. Rothman would find that book, a first edition no less. He'd rally all in his employ—shopkeepers, dock workers, administrators in towering offices—to find it and then he'd bring it to me wrapped in brown paper, as if it were nothing but a small token. No wonder Rothman's been married three times. He knows how to please—until he tires of it.

10.

Dudu Epstein. I couldn't get him out of my head. Dudu Epstein. That *shvitzer.* Have you ever seen a man wear so much jewelry, or smell like he'd been doused in cologne? It was all I could do not to gag when he walked into a room. Soon as Pnina mentioned he'd be at her dinner party, I remembered how I had begged you to tell me why you wrote that damn play, what it meant to you, a woman who forces her staff to bathe their children in indigo dye. She's obsessed with the color, the status it gives her, the extraordinary expense and labor it takes to extract and process. *Aren't they beautiful*, she coos in the second act, running her hands over cherubic arms and legs, cradling them to her—little blue babies, while her own child remains unblemished until that terrible final scene. I wanted to understand where your need to destroy came from. After years of believing that we were a good couple, the perfect artistic couple to our friends, we were hardly talking to each other then. I thought if I understood the origins of your play, I could forgive you for it, for saying that you wrote her for me. Because let's be honest, Max, you wrote her for you as a weapon to use against me.

Still, I believed you when you said it was a metaphor for the war. I asked you to explain. But you couldn't. By then your words had evaporated. You stopped writing. There's an end point to creating, to the imagination, you said, and with *Di Bloy Dame* you had reached yours.

11.

Rothman mentioned you wanted to know what I do all day. Each morning I wake at six to the sound of the nuns praying in the chapel and then it's breakfast. A slice of toast, a runny yolk, a wedge of melon. At 10:00 a.m., Dr. S serves me tea and chocolate wafers. He sits behind his oak desk. Light from the bronze lamp spills onto the blotter where he tucks in his notes about me. Beneath my feet is a plush rug. I remove my shoes without him noticing and sink my toes into the thick pile. Every time he takes a bite of the wafer, crumbs fall onto his shirt. I observe the way his mouth negotiates the sweet. We sip in silence, each taking care not to slurp too loudly. He asks about my career. I tell him about the early roles I played as a young actress in Tel-Aviv, at the beginning of our marriage when we joined the theatrical troupe, *Ha Pleetim—The Refugees*.

How many years were you with them, Dr. S asks.

Three, I say, from 1951 to '53.

He jots down that bit of information and then says, Tell me about your best role.

So I tell him about the artistic director of the Habima theater, who owed Rothman a favor. He gave me the chance to audition for the part of Medea, and to my astonishment, I got it. I remember I could barely contain my excitement, felt almost sick with it, and waited for you to come home from rehearsals. I'd bought a bottle of Fantasia, a cheap sparkling wine, to celebrate and gave you the news the moment you crossed the threshold. You gave me a pained smile, a kiss on the cheek.

Mazel Tov, you said, and then over dinner asked, Is this really what you want?

Of course. How can you even question it?

She's a monster, you said.

Medea was one of my greatest performances, I tell Dr. S. Memorable, according to the critics in all the major papers. You know the play?

I read it in college, he says.

Do you think she's a monster? I ask, my heart

raging in my chest.

Do you?

It's infuriating when he answers a question with a question.

I shrug. I left the world I knew in ruin.

He lights his pipe. You mean the character leaves her world in ruin after she's been betrayed.

His eyes are rheumy, the irises swimming in their sockets like goldfish. He appears older in the morning. His skin is so pale, it's almost blue.

Yes, Doctor. I place my hands in my lap, so he'll know that I'm a cooperative patient, then maybe he'll sign the release forms stashed in his desk and let me go. I want so much to leave here, to return to our apartment on West End Avenue, to resume my life with you, Max.

Who else have you played? Dr. S asks.

Dozens of roles. Maybe hundreds.

Tell me about another.

I would but the pills you've prescribed make me groggy. Can we continue this tomorrow?

He ignores my attempt at deflection and with deft slyness asks, Are you haunted by the roles you've played?

Haunted?

Yes.

Why would I be?

Because Medea kills her children.

My head pounds and my jaw aches. I can't open my mouth for the pain.

Dr. S relents and the orderly escorts me back to my room.

12.

A bad night. A very bad night.

Sister Francoise is an excellent nurse. She prescribes something I've never heard of—hydrotherapy, a remedy for the jumps, to calm the nerves. She leads me down to the basement. The room is like an old cistern, large and musty with a row of four tubs at one end and two showers at the other. It smells of damp wool and pine cleanser. There are no mirrors, only two cracked porcelain sinks along a wall and a frosted window, open enough for me to see the bottom edge of a crescent moon peering through the Aleppo pines in the garden. Sister Francoise removes my nightgown. I try to conceal my nakedness from her; she brushes my hands away and scrubs me down with a bar of soap wrapped in a worn washcloth like my mother used to. Her hands are efficient. They're everywhere.

Thank you, I say when she's done. I'd like to go to bed now.

She says nothing and hoses me down. The water is cool. I shiver and goose bumps erupt on my body. A spool of soapy water swirls down the drain. I imagine Sister Francoise and I caught in the stream, slipping into the pipes that wash out to sea, her habit billowing like a pirate's black sail.

Come on, she says, and leads me to the tub that's covered in a canvas sheet.

She rolls it back. It's filled to the brim with water so hot, vapors rise off the surface. It's like stepping into a cauldron. I cry out, but Sister pays no attention to my distress. When I am fully submerged, the canvas is back in place and keeps my head from sinking. I don't know how long I lie there. Time evaporates. Silence becomes another layer of heat sapping my strength. My bones are liquefied. My mind is empty; my body is empty. Something has been exorcised from it. I am so weak, Sister Francoise needs to lift me out of the tub. She dries me off gently, almost lovingly. My face slides into the curve of her neck. Her wimple catches on my bottom lip.

Now, now, she says, and slips the nightgown over my head. See, all calm, she tucks me into bed.

Yes, Sister, I say.

Everything's fine now. Like nothing ever happened. There's no need for you to worry, Max. I take the bad day and wash it away. Like nothing happened. Isn't that how we do things, *liebchen*? We turn tragedy into comedy and comedy into love affairs, and when we get too old for that, well, here we are—you alone in our apartment in New York and me in the *mishugeh* house in Jaffa.

There's an orderly, a Georgian woman who works for the Sisters. She wears a loud headscarf of questionable taste and must be in her late fifties. She speaks only Gruzinic. You should see her teeth. They're a marvel. The top and bottom rows are crowned in gold. I've seen this only once before in my life, in 1941 in the gulag in Kolyma, the labor camp in Siberia. That mouth belonged to a Polish prisoner named Janusz. Every few months he removed another tooth to pay for goods on the black market—horse meat, loose tea when he could get it, a bar of soap now and then, and Lenya, the camp whore in barracks eight. For a few extra *grushim* she left the curtain open. A peep show on a shoestring budget.

The Georgian woman is proud of her teeth. She bares them constantly. From her pocket comes a key that opens the door to the small balcony in my room. Tomasz must have awakened from his nap, because just as spring washes in, so does Chopin's nocturne. I can smell the chlorophyll rising off the grass and the rain coming in from the north. Remember after we were married how we stood on the balcony during the first rain of the season? Our neighbors screaming at us to get inside, calling us *mishegeneh.* The rain lashing. The sky above a fearsome gray. Our clothes plastered to our skin and we kissing, kissing. God, I loved it when we kissed. I loved your face, your dark blue eyes, the clean ascetic cheeks, the long nose and square chin. I loved how your blond hair bordered on brown and how it curled after we made love.

In this country, rain smells like freedom, you shouted at the sky just as a flash of lightning burst across a cloud.

There are no chairs on the balcony, so the Georgian woman and I lean against the iron railing like those women in Italian movies, greeting the American soldiers who've come to liberate them. The orderly chatters on in Gruzinic. She doesn't mind that I don't understand a word and points to two stray dogs near the rosemary bushes and gives me a salacious wink. It's not the first time I've seen dogs *shtupping*. In the camp, the guards caught a pair in a shed and shot them. The more jovial guard said they should've let them finish before slaughtering them, but the other, more pragmatic one said there was no better time to die, so they'd done them a service. Rothman and I were there when the guards dropped the dogs onto the grass. Their teeth bared, bodies attached mid-coitus, a pair of spooning lovers: the male big spoon, the female little spoon. The guards eviscerated them and said if we cleaned up the mess, they'd give us a serving of stew. Rothman and I buried it all, not a trace left. I was always so hungry, I thought I could eat anything, but it turned out I couldn't. Rothman ate my portion. He gave me his bread.

With the Georgian woman I get to use my miming skills and indicate that we ought to give the dogs their privacy, but she laughs and calls me something in Gruzinic, which I take to mean prudish. We return our attention to the dogs' performance. I admire the female dog. She remains stoic amid all that vigorous humping. Later the Georgian woman tugs at my sleeve and we go inside. She removes her kerchief in a gesture of commiseration and rubs my head.

Maybe Rothman has already told you. They cut my hair, Max. The nuns. Three of them came into my room. I should've known something was up when they locked the door behind them. Did you know they wear gold wedding bands and believe they're married to Jesus? And there's no divorce. Not for them. Sister Francoise is an impressive woman at all times. She's six feet and one inch tall. I know because I looked up her medical record in the file cabinet behind Dr. S's desk when he had to step out during one of our sessions. She towers over us all.

I'm sorry, my dear, Sister Francoise said, but we think vanity may be interfering with your recovery. You should be better by now, more at ease.

I am better, I said. Much better. I wiped the sweat from my palms on my robe and recalled the hydrotherapy session.

I had hoped Dr. S was ready to sign my release form and sent them as emissaries of liberation. Then I saw the shears and understood the Sisters weren't there to free me but were delivering a lesson in humility.

Please, I begged, and promised that from now on I'd wear my hair braided, or cover my head altogether, like my mother before the war when we were pious and didn't mix the *milkhik* with the *fleishik*. They waited for me to plait my hair. My hands shook, so it took some time. What patience these nuns have!

It's true, I said, I take pleasure in brushing my hair. No, *pleasure* is the wrong word. Comfort. I take comfort and comfort isn't vanity, is it? I mean, even when I stand in front of a mirror, I hardly look at myself. Who'd want to see this? I said, drawing an imaginary circle around my face like some amateur comedian at Grossinger's angling for a laugh. I got nothing, not a chuckle, not a smile, not even a quivering lip.

Sister Francoise bowed her head. I think she said a prayer in Latin or maybe it was French, then snapped the scissors open and shut like a pair of canine jaws. She pressed the cold blade against my neck and just like that it was done. What had taken years of tending, coloring, straightening, the chemical relaxers doing their best to iron out the Yiddish kink, the weekly shampoo at the salon on

75th, roasting under the dryers, listening to the blue-haired ladies yelling about whose bris they'd attended and what fish was served, disappeared in seconds.

Dr. S was furious with them. But what could he do?

Don't worry, it'll grow back, he patted the inch or so of hair the good Sisters left on my head.

Now whenever my reflection catches in the window, I think, I know her, I've seen her before.

13.

The first time I saw the Georgian woman, I was sure that I recognized her; she looked so familiar. I woke in a strange room. The window was shuttered. I made my way to the door in the dark, but it was locked. There was a cot in the corner. I rested there, waiting for someone to release me. I smelled smoke and the sound of fabric burning filled my head and then the Georgian woman entered. Her hair was braided in a crown, and when she opened her mouth to speak, the light caught on her gold teeth. Her hands jerked agitatedly over her uniform before she stuffed them into her pockets.

"Do I know you?" I said, but she was already moving down the hall. I felt I'd been locked in that room for days, maybe weeks. I was thirsty and had to relieve myself but there was no toilet, only a chamber pot under the cot that I couldn't bring myself to use. And then I remembered where I'd seen the Georgian woman before or someone like her, because even in my befuddled state I knew she couldn't be the matron from the children's home in Kolyma who also wore her hair in a braided crown. Each week I stood in line with the other children stripped down to our underwear, shivering, waiting for her to shave our heads to rid us of the lice that feasted on us while the snow and wind smacked against the orphanage walls.

We called her the Queen of Razor Blades. She scraped our scalps with a straight razor, nicking the sores left from last week's sweep. I always tried to be first in line when the razor was sharpest. Cuts were deeper when it wasn't. Rothman taught me that. And because I raced to the front of the line and didn't hang back like the others, the matron thought I was a good and eager comrade and made me responsible for the orphaned toddlers. I had to make sure they were washed and fed and didn't get underfoot. For this I received an extra ration of bread a week.

The matrons were a surly lot, each with a switch in their hands, and if they couldn't find a branch, a shoe did just as well, a belt if they had one. I didn't hold the children. I didn't sing to them or play with them. I was eight at the start of the war. I barely spoke to anyone, except for Rothman and my mother. My mother visited the Children's Home for a few hours on Sunday afternoons. It was her only time off from her duties as a laundress. I chattered like a small bird as she fed me a potato, sometimes a beet. Those first months I learned all the children's names: Roza, Micha, Tzila, Shmulik, Wolfe, Basya, Shlomo, Baruch, but after that winter when so many died of pneumonia, I stopped. The last winter in the camp I didn't even bother numbering them. I made sure they were fed and washed, but no more than that. Five years of war had turned us all into wolves. And the leader of the wolves was Rothman. He taught me to survive, to steal, to lie. Like him, I'd have done anything for a bowl of barley soup and a heel of bread.

When I am alone in my room, I search for the treats the Georgian woman leaves behind: cigarettes, a matchbook, a fifth of Smirnoff, a bar of Elite chocolate. She finds the cash Rothman gives me, smuggled in my shoe, and takes more than we agreed on. It's worth it. I smoke a cigarette in my bathroom, sip the vodka, and feel the heat travel the length of my throat and wash up in my belly. I smoke half a cigarette and save the rest for later. All of this gives me a sense of déjà vu.

14.

A conversation with Dr. S the same week the nuns cut my hair:

Tell me what the New York critics said about your Yiddish Jocasta, he says while trying not to stare at my sorry head.

How did you hear about that? May I? I point to the cigarette box on his desk. It's something a child has made with tongue depressors and glue. A grandchild, perhaps?

He nods. I looked you up, he says, and strikes a match.

I'm flattered, I say, puffing on the cigarette.

Jocasta, he urges.

An excellent part for a woman my age. I take a deep drag and blow a train of smoke above my head.

And? he says.

You know the story. What she does to her child.

Remind me?

Tomasz is in fine form. The strains of the nocturne burble under Dr. S's door. I wonder if our resident pianist is wearing his brown-and-white-striped pajamas today.

Well? he says.

In her attempt to save her son, she destroys him, I say.

And?

Everything else follows.

15.

You placed an ad in the *Jewish Press* a few weeks before I left New York, and put it on your desk for me to find. I know things were bad between us, but how could you do it, Max? *Nischt eyns vort.* Not one word about it. The advertisement as blunt as a brick: Apartment for sale. The Street of Shoes, Number 9, Apartment 6, Tel Aviv, Israel.

What were you thinking? What would selling our home in Tel Aviv accomplish? You don't need the money so why would you get rid of the one place we were truly happy?

Rothman told me you asked for his help.

Nischt eyns vort. Not one word from you to mark this betrayal.

16.

In the dream I am in an interrogation room at a police station near the Twin Towers. The detective is a woman I've never met. She switches on a reel-to-reel tape player that sounds like ribbons tied to the spokes of a child's bicycle and states for the record that it's 3:47 a.m. Her hair is blue and sits on her head like a helmet. An officer in full regalia guards the door. Rothman is beside me in a pinstriped suit, acting as my attorney. He wears his expensive gold watch and checks it every few minutes. Wife number three is young and restless, waiting for him at home. He is anxious to get to her. She sleeps with a packed suitcase under the bed. It rests there like a warning, a signal that she could leave him at a moment's notice. What reason does she give, I ask Rothman. He counts off, one, disappointment; two, unhappiness; three, boredom. And for this he almost loves her, for this and the daughter she's given him, like a gift, a most perfect gift.

The interrogation begins and the three speak in a language I don't understand, and though you aren't in the room, I hear you say to me that it's Aramaic.

How do you know?

My father taught me.

But that language is dead.

Like us, you said.

Rothman turns to me and smiles. The right half of his mouth is crowned in gold, but it's the left side, where the teeth are shattered, and the jaw has caved in that I cannot stop looking at.

17.

I miss reading the newspaper. Rothman isn't any good at giving me the day's news. To him, everything is fleeting and so why bother dwelling on events that will change nothing or everything. The only things worth knowing are those that affect his livelihood. Do you remember the biblical scholar who lived next door? For an entire year before he and his wife abandoned New York for Jerusalem, he stole our newspaper every morning. In the afternoon on my way to the theater, I'd run into him in the elevator. He was always garbed in a worsted suit, shoes shined. The *mamzer* had the nerve to tip his hat and say, How are you today? I'd reply, Well, and you, and ask after his wife. We'd go on this way politely, a smugness playing around his mouth, a fury in my chest, choking me as I thought of him reading our paper over his breakfast, while you or I had to run down to Stein's to purchase a new one, convinced that our newspaper, the one we had ordered, never arrived. You didn't believe it was him, someone so erudite, a *yekke* like you, until the morning I woke you at 5:30 a.m. and we waited by the peephole and watched him tiptoe to our door dressed in a burgundy velour robe and slippers that I'd seen on sale at Bonwit Teller. I was dismayed when you shrugged your shoulders and went back to bed and knew that you wouldn't confront him or demand that he pay for the papers he'd pilfered from us.

One evening while you were teaching your course on Yiddish writers at Stern College, his door was ajar and I looked in and saw him sitting in the living room, enjoying the radio and reading our Yiddish paper, *Forverts.* That fury in my chest returned with such force that I ran back to our apartment and grabbed the first sharp instrument I could find; it happened to be an ice pick. I saw his Volvo parked in its usual spot in the garage, and I punctured all four of his tires. I'd never done anything like that before. It was exhilarating. Rothman would have approved. He thrives on vengeance. You would have been horrified. It was so much easier than I'd imagined. I left the ice pick on his welcome mat. After that, no matter what time we rose, our paper was there, neatly folded on the doorstep, and he tipped his hat, the smugness gone from his face, only a fearful awareness remained that I was a stranger to him, a danger he hadn't counted on.

18.

In my dream, Rothman asks me how I hurt my hands. Hurt? I repeat and look to see that both are wrapped in bandages. I unwind a mile of gauze, and the closer I get to the skin, the more my hands burn. A blister sits in the center of each palm the size of a snow globe, and inside the dome of my right hand is a miniature version of me, and inside the dome of my left hand is a miniature version of you. We are swimming back and forth from one end to the other, unable to stop, doomed to perform this act for eternity.

You smell of smoke, Rothman says.

He's right, my clothes stink. There's soot under my fingernails and nothing to relieve the pain in my hands.

"Can you tell us what led to the events at Number 9, the Street of Shoes?" the detective asks. The tape continues to churn.

19.

Crows swoop in and out of the Aleppo pines that border the garden. Dr. S pours tea into porcelain china cups. My mother had a similar set when we lived in Krosniewice before the war. The rims were decorated in gold with a chain of yellow primroses beneath. Every afternoon she'd brew a pot of Darjeeling a relative from England sent us for Rosh Hashanah. She would place a cube of sugar in the center of the cup, then pour the tea over it. After the sugar dissolved and the tea was stirred, she would float a paper-thin slice of lemon on the surface, so thin it was almost transparent. I was fascinated by the graceful movement of her hands during what became a kind of ceremonial ritual we shared, the way she lifted the sugar tongs, then submerged her spoon into the brew and rotated it counterclockwise without ever scraping the sides of the cup. No one had more elegant hands than my mother. She took great care of them. On Thursday evenings when my father worked late at his butcher shop, we'd listen to a concert on the radio and she'd dip her hands into a pot of melted paraffin wax, then hold them in the air while I wrapped them in warm towels. I loved cracking open the hardened wax casing, revealing the soft pink and white flesh beneath. The impression of her lifeline and whorls on her fingertips embedded in the wax were like a map of a secret city. All my life I tried to decipher the mystery that was my mother. She smelled of roses and old books, silver polish, and yeast. I didn't know much about her past. In my childish mind she was born the moment I was. We'd sip our tea, sometimes blowing gently to cool it. She'd ask about my school day and I'd recount in detail what I had learned, still wearing the red plaid uniform with the gold crest on the pocket. Even then I was good at recitation and the teacher would commend me in front of the class. I loved the world of words, the feel of them gliding off my tongue and how my voice would make them ring and tremble. My performance made even the children who knocked me down and spat the word *zhyd*, Jew, in the schoolyard sit up in their chairs. At the end, everyone clapped. For those few minutes, I was beloved. I was one of them. That same sense of belonging envelops me every time an audience applauds.

After our tea, Mama and I would walk along the lakeshore. She'd point out the blue heron hidden in the reeds. I imagined climbing onto its back and taking flight, its neck stretching, its wings expanding wide, flying high above our town, over the main square where farmers sold their produce on market days. The church and its towering cross puncturing the sky and the Jewish quarter with our modest synagogue, not far from my father's butcher shop. Beyond was the forest where we were told never to go. Not a good place for Jews—too dark, too many trees, too many acres into which we could disappear.

In winter, Mama and I would bundle up and skate on the lake, sometimes Papa closed his shop early and joined us, and if the sun shone, we'd see heaven reflected in the ice. When Rothman and Tomasz were there, Mama would stand on the bank watching the three of us glide across the clouds, her elegant hands buried in a fox fur muff. She sold the muff for bread and potatoes in one of the towns we stopped in during the long journey to Siberia. By then Krosniewice was overtaken by the German army and a ghetto was created for the Jewish families that remained.

What brought you to Israel? Dr. S asks.

The weather, I say. New York can be brutal in winter.

20.

The next day Dr. S continues with the same line of questioning.

Tell me what you hoped to find here? he says.

In the hospice?

Israel.

What do you mean?

Why did you leave your home?

I gaze out the window at the garden. Have you ever noticed how palm trees resemble conductors, I say, short and squat, tall and thin, all with floppy hair, conducting a symphony no one can hear?

Dr. S is disappointed in me. I thought we'd moved beyond this, he says, then calls for the orderly.

What should I tell him, Max? That we fought? That

at the age of sixty-six I left the desert of our marriage and moved across the world into the apartment we'd abandoned forty-three years ago? Do I reveal that I couldn't live in our continent of loneliness another day? Or do I resort to the banal, tell him my flight from New York to Tel-Aviv was long and arduous, that we flew into an unexpected snowstorm that grounded us in Brussels for twenty hours? You have no idea how humiliating it is to sit alone in that overly bright terminal devouring one order of *pomme-frites* after another, as passengers dressed in leisurewear buy bottles of untaxed booze and bricks of Côte d'Or chocolates. As if that wasn't enough, I ate a tube of marzipan the size of my forearm. What a *chazer* I made of myself.

How can I confess to him before I confess to you that I flirted shamelessly with a stranger, a man whose barrel chest and coarse face reminded me of the jolly camp guard who slaughtered those poor dogs. We sat at the airport bar drinking, his thick fingers strangling a tumbler of J&B, the pinky nail on his right hand as long as a hawk's talon. I was dizzy drunk. The ground shifted beneath me. I excused myself and took extra care not to stumble on my way to the bathroom. It had just been cleaned and was empty, the floor still damp, the air crimped with Pine-Sol. He followed me in and pushed me into a stall. I didn't object. We barely looked at each other, both of us long past our prime. But the body remembers its uses, how to fuck, how to yield. His sweat smelled of onions. Afterward, I found myself on the freshly mopped floor. My underwear around my ankles, a spot of blood on my thigh. I don't know how I reached the gate. By the time I arrived at Ben Gurion Airport in Tel Aviv, I was sick to my stomach and feverish with exhaustion.

21.

Rothman stopped by today. He found a buyer for the apartment. He brought the sales contract and wanted me to sign it. We argued. Sister Francoise marched him out of the ward. He left the contract behind. I tore it to pieces then took a match to it. Tomorrow he'll bring another. The man is relentless. You really shouldn't have done it, Max.

22.

I spend the morning watching the boys in the *Collège des Frères,* my face crushed against the glass. A cry goes up, a small boy falls to his knees. The others rush to his side and lift him to his feet.

My heart swells to see such kindness in children.

23.

Dr. S lights his pipe of cherry tobacco. Tell me about your husband.

Max?

He nods and offers me a cigarette.

I'd rather smoke your pipe, I say. It smells delicious.

He chuckles, then in a firm voice repeats, Your husband.

I listen to the Sisters sweep through the hall on rubber soles, the winglike swish of their habits as they pass the door to Dr. S's office. Soon Tomasz will play the nocturne and the Georgian woman will walk me back to my room. There's still the chocolate left to eat and vodka to drink in my stash of contraband.

24.

There's a picture of Dr. S's wife on his desk. May I see it?

He turns the frame toward me and bites the tip of his pipe, brow furrowed.

She is beautiful, dark-haired, brown-eyed, an easy smile. Much younger than him, so she must be the second or third wife because he also has a photograph of a young man graduating medical school.

Is that your son?

He nods and then asks, Can you tell me about your marriage?

I return the frame to the desk. The day is overcast and a gray pall spreads like lighter fluid into the room.

I have a headache, I say, and close my eyes. My face drains of color. Did you know I could still do that? I use Stanislavsky's sense memory technique and recall a time when I felt great dread. I think of Rothman's accident in the forest in the camp when he swung an axe to fell a tree and cut his thigh. He was so weak and in horrible pain. I sat with him six, seven weeks, maybe more, and didn't leave his side until he recovered his strength. At the time, no one thought he'd survive and, if he did, he'd never walk again. But this was Rothman, and I came to believe he could do anything. I think of that day, his terrible cry echoing through the pines, and my throat fills with bile. My heart races. I go into a cold sweat and my face blanches.

Dr. S calls for the Georgian woman, who stands outside the door ready to escort me to my room.

Maybe later, he says, as I stand to leave. When you feel up to it.

Yes, all right, I say.

She gives me a pill that makes me sleepy and I crawl into my nun's cot, feeling the thick fingers of the Belgian on my neck.

25.

In the taxi from the airport to our apartment in Tel Aviv, I smell the Belgian's sour mash on my skin. The strains of a Mizrahi love song washes through the cab. We pass a sleepy farming village where a tractor crouches like a spider in a field. Prickly pear line the road, their thorny leaves the size of place mats. The pastoral gives way to industry, then to urban sprawl, to billboards advertising Rolex watches and Ahava cosmetics. A heavy mist drenches the evening sky, dampening the road, condensing on the windows. My empty face reflected there.

The night before I left New York, you said I was a golem who left you without love or children. I took particular care not to look at you then. I knew that, like me, you were remembering the winter we lost Asher to bronchopneumonia. Our boy who completed us, healed us, who filled the world between the *nischt ahin, nischt aher* with light and joy. Nine months old. How could a body that small house something as large as our future?

I was twenty-three. You were twenty-five. Our careers were just beginning. I don't know how we survived those first years without him. But we finally reached a point when his death was no longer the subtext in our conversations. We stopped hearing his labored breaths in our dreams, stopped seeing the oxygen tent in our minds, the silent figures in the room, checking and rechecking valves and measuring blood and oxygen levels. We stopped listening for the beep of the heart monitor and we let go of the prayers. *Tseyt khilz.* Time heals, or maybe it only obscures.

After Asher's death, we grew an extra layer of skin over our eyes, a lizard membrane that protected and blinded, enabling us to maneuver out of the way what we didn't want to see. For people whose religion is guilt, it was our only path forward. For years I woke up parched with the names of the dead in my mouth, certain Asher's passing was my punishment for neglecting the toddlers in the children's home in Kolyma who'd come crying half frozen to my bed at night. I'd send them back to their cots, afraid to love them, afraid to lose them.

So much had been lost already. I had room in my heart then only for Rothman, who refused to let me wither, for my mother, who hung on as long as she could, and my father, who'd been drafted into Stalin's army almost from the moment we had crossed into the Soviet Union. He barely caught his breath before they gave him a uniform two sizes too big, stained with another man's blood.

I couldn't forgive myself for Asher's death and you couldn't forgive me. There was no talk of having another child, though I desperately wanted one. We couldn't even work up the energy to leave each other, to find comfort elsewhere, to start fresh with someone new. No, we committed ourselves to a life sentence, to enshrining what we'd lost, to never forgetting. You encouraged me to work, and so I took on more roles, no matter how small, but you need to know that each character I played was Asher, and each story was us, and each night I told you in the only way I knew that I loved you and that in your face I saw our boy and in him I saw the boy you were.

And you loved me too, Max, no matter how many distractions you had—your students, your actresses. Every female character you wrote was me. From the moment we met, until *Di Bloy Dame*, until you saw Rothman's tiny daughter sitting on the rug in our living room, tugging off her socks, playing with her toes. I saw your smile waver. I felt your body collapse, as if the scaffold that had held you up all those years had given way.

26.

In our next meeting, Dr. S turns on the lamp and rummages through the drawers in his desk, banging them loudly, growing more frustrated. The fuss makes me nervous. I feel my stomach knot. When he's done combing through a sheaf of papers, he pins me with a look.

Why did you leave your husband? He barks the question.

He's caught me by surprise, but before I can respond, a siren pierces the ward. Dr. S jumps to his feet. He is called away on an emergency.

Sister Francoise shuttles me to my room.

What happened? I say, the beating hands of panic in my chest.

Nothing for you to worry about. She has my elbow in a vise grip, but I manage to turn around and see a gurney being wheeled into the sunroom.

The beeping finally stops, and an unremitting silence curdles the ward. I clutch Sister Francoise's hand.

Is he all right?

The image of Tomasz, the boy who fell into the lake with flat-planed stones in his pockets, perfect for skipping, floats past me.

With God's grace, she says, and tugs on her wimple.

27.

The following day I ask Dr. S about Tomasz the pianist.

You know I can't discuss other patients with you.

At least tell me if he's alive.

Of course he's alive.

Will he play again?

Dr. S examines a scuff on his shoe and frowns. Probably. Eventually.

But you aren't sure? What happened to his hands?

What makes you think something happened to his hands? His eyes pin me to the chair.Well, he must have done something to them. I squeeze my knees together. It's so quiet now. I shiver to prove to Dr. S that the silence is uncanny.

He clears his throat. So, it's Henrik you're

worried about?

Who?

Our resident pianist.

Is that his name? I thought it was Tomasz.

Who's Tomasz?

No one, I say.

After a few minutes he murmurs, Why don't we begin.

Begin?

He shakes his head. Coyness doesn't suit you. We were talking about your marriage, remember?

My eyes skid across his desk. The picture of his young wife is missing. I look out onto the garden. The gladioli are in bloom and the long tendril-like aerial roots of the banyan tree sweep the ground. Dr. S waits for me to speak. He sighs and Sister Francoise appears. She holds my hand, and we walk through the corridor. The rosaries that hang at her waist swing from side to side.

28.

You left the milk out on the counter last summer after the play closed, knowing I couldn't bear to see food go to waste. It soured and I begged you not to pour it down the drain, but you did.

I could have used it in a cake or biscuit mix, like buttermilk, I said. I could have scalded it.

No, it's spoiled, you said. The shadow of a smile hovered over your lips.

I understood then that we'd crossed a boundary. I told you that in the camp I carried a tin bowl with me everywhere. Anyone who lost their bowl starved. We wore it round our necks. Rothman used a nail and the heel of his boot to puncture a hole near the rim and ran a length of wire through it that turned my neck green. I bathed with it, slept with it. I never let it go, not even after the war when Rothman and I went back to Krosniewice in search of our relatives and neighbors. We found strangers in our houses. Strangers who used our furniture and hung our curtains on the windows. They ate the stores of food we left in the cellar off of our china plates. They dug up the candlesticks, the jewelry, the coins, and the silver *kiddush* cup we'd buried in the garden before we left. No one we knew was alive. When we knocked on our front doors, hoping for a familiar face, when we peered through the windows into our parlors, they chased us off like we were dogs come begging for a meal and warned that if we came back, they'd murder us. We'd heard stories in other towns of Jews who'd returned to their homes after the war, only to be beaten dead by people who had once been their neighbors. Rothman said it was because they didn't want to give back what they'd stolen from us. But I think it was because we'd dared to survive. Live Jews are a nuisance.

It was his idea to obtain visas to Israel. We had kicked around Poland for two years. It was 1948 and we were orphans. Rothman said Europe had spit us out once; he wasn't going to give them a chance to do it again. Unlike you, instead of being placed on a kibbutz where we might have learned to dig a ditch or plant a fruit tree, Rothman lied and said we had relatives in Tel Aviv. He'd had enough of communal living in the gulag, he said, and so for a time we lived on the Tel Aviv-Jaffa border in a *ma'abarah*, a transit camp, a colony of corrugated tin huts the government built for people like us—rootless shadow figures who'd washed up on the Mediterranean shore. We were there two months when Rothman declared that Israel was our home now. We were fed, housed, given jobs. In the morning we studied Hebrew in an *Ulpan* and in the afternoon we worked. I, in Baruch's shoe factory near the central bus station on Neve Sha'anan Street, known as the Street of Shoes, and Rothman as a custodian in Barclay's Bank on Allenby Street, but that job lasted only a few weeks. He didn't have the temperament for it.

On Friday afternoons we walked through old Jaffa, treading on the cobblestones Richard the Lionhearted and Saladin had walked. We saw toothless beggars with their hands outstretched, and rich merchants garbed in linen and silk. We bartered for goods in the souk. Along the waterfront, warehouses were packed with crates of oranges on their way to Europe and America. The city was a rush of color, heat, scent, and sounds. We'd never been anywhere as alive, not even in the marketplaces in Europe before or after the war, and we'd never seen so many different kinds of people in one place. We explored the streets of Tel Aviv, where the white splendor of the Bauhaus buildings glistened in the sunshine, and we gaped at the packed sidewalk cafés, where people kibitzed over *kafe* and a *shtikl kuchin*.

Rothman said it was time to bury the war and so we had to bury our bowls. We filled them with the names of our dead. My mother, who'd died of heart failure, my father in battle. Rothman's sister, who had raised him after the deaths of their parents in a boating accident, and the *kinder,* the children whose voices I heard in my sleep. We buried our bowls in Gan Meir Park in the center of Tel Aviv. We used them to dig a hole in the ground and left them and our childhood beside a row of eucalyptus trees. Afterward, we went to Landwer's café and ordered iced coffee and ate a dozen cinnamon rugelach until we were full enough to burst. I wanted to weep. I wanted to vomit. Rothman saw the flurry of emotions in my face and shook his head in warning. *Not here*, he seemed to say, *not in public, where people can see your weakness, because they'll take advantage of you if they do.* I drew in a breath and pulled myself together. When it was time to pay, he took fifty lira from his pocket, an enormous sum for us then. I knew enough not to ask where he'd gotten the money. At night Rothman snuck out when he thought I was asleep. In the camp, and when we kicked about in Krosniewice, and later in Warsaw, I noticed the way men looked at him, at his lush dark curls, the soft brown eyes, the long, elegant line of his back. Even starving he was beautiful. He'd hang a knowing smile on his face, all of him an invitation, all of him hunger, and the next morning we'd have a bit more bread, a cup of milk, sometimes even an egg.

In the *ma'abarah*, I followed him out and watched him cross Ha Yarkon Street toward the beach, where men waited beside the rocks, their cries drowning in the sea. From one to the other he went, passed around like a used doll. When it was done and the men left to seek their beds and families, Rothman shed his clothes and walked into the water. I waited for him on the beach, worried one day he'd relent and allow the current to carry him the way it had carried Tomasz, but he always returned to me and without a word took my hand. We'd stroll through the city, whose heart we were coming to love, the sky just beginning to show signs of a new day.

At Landwers café, Rothman paid the bill with his fifty-lira note, then tucked my arm through his. We passed the eucalyptus trees where we had buried our bowls. Neither of us looked back.

Max, you left the milk on the counter and then, when it soured, poured it down the drain. I retaliated by staying out without calling, sometimes all night, knowing that each time I didn't phone or come home, you'd relive the day your mother left to buy *schokokuss*, your favorite chocolate and marshmallow confection at Shumann's Konditoria, a quick ride on the trolley from your apartment in Berlin. You were nine, precocious, and had insisted. You needed to have it, and because she loved you and wanted to please you, and because your father, an eminent pediatrician, had been scooped up a few months earlier in the Juni-Aktion, the "June Special," and sent to Buchenwald for what amounted to a traffic violation, she put on her good coat and calf-skinned gloves, her cloche hat, and waved goodbye. Her last words to you were, *Wait for me, my little king.* And you did.

You were a good son. You waited all day and the next too, by the window where you could see her turn the corner onto your street, where you saw the fires in the city and heard the storefronts shatter. With each hour your dread rose like floodwater. The following day your uncle came to take you home. You were faint from hunger, gripping the windowsill, nose pressed to the glass. You had not left your post. From then on, you were known as Max. No one was allowed to call you by the name your mother had given you, *Melech*, King.

29.

Sister Francoise takes me into the garden, where the sun is bright and clings to each blade of grass. Come, she says, and seats me at a small table beneath the banyan tree in the center of the garden, where the pilgrims used to eat their breakfast. On either side of the small gravel path are beds of purple and white lupine. Their heads shake in greeting as we brush past them. The garden walls are draped in ivy. On the other side of the wall is the *Collège des Frères.* The boys are playing baseball in the yard. Shouts and sounds of running feet float into the garden. With bases loaded and a hard thwack of the bat, the ball arcs into the sky and lands at my feet like an offering. I turn to Sister Francois.

Would you like to give it back to them? she asks.

I am overcome. My face breaks into a smile. Yes, Sister, I would.

She removes a latchkey from a hidden pocket in her habit, pulls back the curtain of ivy to reveal an iron door I hadn't known was there. A clutch of boys, ages eight to twelve, waits anxiously, shuffling their feet, staring at the ground, sheepish faces red from exertion. It's obvious this isn't the first time they've lost their ball in the hospice's garden. They bow when they see Sister Francoise the way my classmates and I bowed in respect to our teachers when they'd entered the classroom. She nods in my direction and I approach the threshold, holding the ball in the palm of my hand. The boys stare at me. I am a curiosity, but none of the fear and distaste that I saw in Rothman's daughter appear in their faces. They are used to the likes of us, the desolate and disenchanted, refugees of a lost continent.

I smooth my hair, forlorn at its length. It's still so very short, thanks to Sister Francoise's shears. I don't want to tell her that I feel more vain now knowing how *miskedik* I look than when I had long hair.

Here you go, I say in Hebrew and then in English, giving the ball to a boy whose coal- black waves tumble onto his forehead.

He pushes a hank of hair out of his eyes. Thank you, he says and bows with a quick bob, gripping the ball to his chest.

You're welcome, young man, I say, and search his face, wondering if I'll see a resemblance to someone I know.

When Rothman and I were in Krosniewice after the war, I caught glimpses of my mother in the faces of women in the market and on the bus. She was there in the soft curve of another's cheek, the tilt of a head. And when Rothman and I first arrived in Israel, I saw her strolling down Rothschild Boulevard, pushing a baby carriage. Phantom images of her were everywhere. The shattered fragments of those we know are all around us. I remember after Tomasz was gone, I was distraught and asked my father what happens to us when we die.

For such an important question, we need lots of space and air, he said.

And so, we walked around the lake near where Tomasz had drowned. It was a cold day in early spring. I could hardly feel my feet. My father pulled a reed out of the water and snapped it in two, then showed me its hollow length.

We are all vessels, he said, like this reed. Only we're filled with light, and when we die, the vessel breaks and our light travels into the universe, where it bursts into a thousand pieces, ascending into the world between heaven and earth, where nothing is ever forgotten.

What happens to them, Papa?

He waved his hands up and down and back and forth, mimicking the movement of the shards of light he said floated in the ether alongside the particles of a million souls, and over time, maybe decades or centuries, they find each other, cling to one another, and create new souls born into new bodies.

Does that mean we're stars in the sky until we're born? I asked.

No, stars are stars. We're the light that can't be seen. No one is ever truly gone. All of us are part of each other. Now Tomasz will be too, he said.

When I look at this boy, I see a child who was in the labor camp, an orphan whose name I don't recall, but who had the same gold flecks in his eyes. The matrons had arranged an adoption for him. A middle-aged couple, farmers, I think, picked him up. I don't know where they took him. I don't know if he survived the war. All I remember is watching him step into a small van and disappearing. Yet here he was again in this boy from the *Collège des Frères*—small, agile, and smiling.

All right, boys, back to your game, Sister Francoise says. I'll see you in class tomorrow morning.

Thank you, Sister, they shout, and dash into the yard, past the burbling fountain to where they've left their bats and gloves.

Sister Francoise and I return to the garden, where we sit on a bench in the shade of the banyan tree until it's time for lunch.

30.

One freezing night in late November, before you moved into the spare room, I found you staring out the dining room window facing West End Avenue. Great sheets of black ice covered the road. A phalanx of cars sped past, honking their horns in celebration of a sporting event, flags snapping on their antennas. We heard the terrible skid and then the crash. There was glass everywhere. A woman stumbled out of a car in the middle of the pileup, bleeding down the side of her face. *Where is she?* The cry reached us on the fifth floor. We were high enough to see the entirety of the street. The child, maybe four or five, thrown clear out of her mother's car onto the crumbled fender of another farther ahead, pinned by a jagged piece of metal through her chest. We couldn't look at each other. Something unspeakable had broken between us.

You howled and the sound cracked us wide open, exposing everything we'd buried and burned along the way.

It's all right, Max. The girl will be all right, I said, realizing I'd spent years protecting you from such things, protecting you from me, from who I was and didn't dare become.

You lifted your hands, warding me off as if you suddenly saw me, as if the metaphoric skin that had grown over your eyes had peeled away. Your vision returned.

I know, you shouted, and backed into the wall, slapping your head and face, over and over, beating yourself, trying to dislodge what you'd seen.

Max! I attempted to grab hold of your hands, but you pushed me to the ground, and I lay there stupefied, certain that I had already lived this moment in a dream or a play.

He wasn't my son, you said. He was never my son.

The air grew thin. I couldn't take a full breath and looked up at you wide-eyed. What are you talking about?

She looks just like him, like Asher.

Who?

Rothman's little girl. I saw it the summer they

were here.

I shook my head, as if to clear it. That was almost a year ago. Why didn't you say anything?

You'd have denied it. Your eyes squeezed shut and then you walked away from me.

Max, Max, I called, stricken, but you were already gone, left the apartment without your coat.

That night when you returned half-frozen, white-lipped, your cheeks windburned, you moved your things into the study. Only the scent of you remained in the bed sheets.

Ten days we didn't speak, sealed within the walls of our prewar apartment. A kind of catatonia set in. I had no *cheshek* for anything, no desire at all. I called the theater, whispered to the house manager that I was sick, voiceless. I had never missed a performance in my life. But I thought, How could I possibly go onstage when your accusation, for that's what it was, consumed me?

You left to teach your class. I scoured your room for clues, ideas, anything that would help me understand how you came to such a conclusion when Rothman's daughter looked nothing like our son. I found nothing. I wrapped myself in your blanket on the sofa, sat in the big leather chair at your desk, and that's when I saw the advertisement in the *Jewish Press* for the sale of our apartment in Tel Aviv. I felt a kind of terror and knew that my life, the one you and I took such pains to construct, was in terrible danger. Then as if to prove it, I found two envelopes under the newspaper and tore them open. The first had the seal of the New York State Supreme Court, where you'd petitioned for divorce two months before the accident on West End Avenue. The second, embossed with the seal of the *Bais Din*, the New York Rabbinate, was more recent. You had applied for a *Get*, a divorce decree, without telling me.

The night before I left, you came into my bedroom, your face waxy with fright. I hoped that you had come to your senses. I hoped that we could forgive each other. But the only words you said to me were, *I dreamed I was the little king.*

31.

I ask Sister Francoise if I can visit Tomasz-Henrik. She's pleased and says that I show true Christian charity. We walk to the far end of the ward to his room and find him in bed, looking out the window at a stretch of sky so blue, my throat aches at the sight of it. He's tucked beneath the sheets, his arms pale against the bedding. I expected them to be muscular from playing the piano; instead they're spindly and whittled like branches stripped of their bark. Both wrists are bandaged and two fingers on his right hand are in splints. I imagine he slammed the fallboard on them and wonder at his ingenuity, his use of the piano wire on his wrists, how deep it must have cut. A bruise escapes the bandages and rivers upstream toward his elbow.

Go ahead, Sister Francoise says.

Afraid to startle him, I clear my throat, an innocuous sound to which he reacts with a violent shudder. A blank stare in my direction. His eyes never quite land on my face. To Tomasz-Henrik, I am a mosaic. When he's pieced me together, recognition lights his eyes. His face splits into a wide grin.

Rivkaleh, he shouts with glee, Rivkah, *ketzeleh.*

His wounded hands shake as he speaks and then he sobs, a terrible sob that splinters the air. Sister Francoise mumbles something under her breath and hustles me out of the room, forgetting to lock the door behind her. She marches me down the hall, my elbow cupped in her hand. Her *couvrechef* whips behind us.

Who is Rivkaleh?

His first wife, Sister Francoise says.

Is she alive?

Sister shakes her head. She died in Kutno. Typhus, I think. He was there when they loaded her onto the wagon. Poor woman.

There's a nurses' station in the center of the ward.

"May I have a bit of Scotch tape?" I say.

"What for?"

"An aerogram has lost its glue."

Sister Francoise gives me the roll and reminds me to return it. That afternoon while the Georgian woman retrieves the cash from my shoe, I place three strips of tape, one over the other, on the bolt to keep it from locking. Such a small thing and yet my heart races. I imagine my escape, flying past the nurses' station, down the corridor, the entrance wide open, the sisters sealed in the chapel during Vespers, begging the *Eyn Sof*, the eternal one, for mercy. But when darkness falls and all is quiet, I sneak past the sleeping sister on duty and walk the hall like a ghost. I am nothing. I am weightless. I reach the entrance but cannot bring myself to step out. The rush of cars on the road terrifies me. The thought of being swallowed up in the darkness alone haunts me. I am in a panic. My heart pounds so hard, my chest hurts. Instead, I run to Tomasz-Henrik's door and turn the knob, trembling, happy to find it still unlocked. There's an almost imperceptible creak when I step inside, to which his sensitive musician's ear is attuned. His eyes flutter open. Rivkaleh? His voice is full of wonder. He makes room for me on the bed. We hold each other; our breath fills the lonely space between us. I am calm again. The bones of his rib cage insistent against my breasts. In that moment, I am his wife. I am Rivkaleh and it is such a relief to be someone else again. I whisper to him, *You are my little king.* He hums the nocturne in my ear. We sleep, and when dawn arrives, I slip out of his bed. Tomasz-Henrik watches me go, frowning.

Who are you? he says.

No one, I reply.

32.

The cabdriver pulls up to the curb on the Street of Shoes, across from the old central bus station in Tel Aviv.

You sure this is the address? Number 9? he says in a thick Moroccan accent.

Yes. I sit in the cab wrapped in the evening light, shivering with excitement. The dim glow of the streetlamp spills onto the pavement. The Street of Shoes is shabbier than I remember. Baruch's shoe Factory on the corner where I once worked is now a restaurant that sells falafel and shawarma. There's still the outline of a slingback shoe on a faded sign, and the scent of glue is a knot of memory that won't let go.

Maybe a hotel? I take you. No charge. This place is no good, the driver says.

I open the door and he exhales a swift curse,

one of those expressive Arabic curses Rothman and I picked up in our first weeks in the country back in '48. *Koos emak*, the driver hisses, then lumbers out of the car. He removes my suitcase from the trunk. The street is littered with the day's garbage; piles of it slouch against the lampposts. A tall, emaciated man lurches toward Levinsky Park a few blocks away, his shadow stretching long behind him.

The driver shakes his head. The place is full of heroin addicts, he says. One of them could rob you, rape you, or worse. Wouldn't you rather be in a nice clean hotel?

What's that? I point to a blue light flashing outside a bungalow a few blocks away.

Probably a *Beit zonot*, you know, a brothel, he says.

There's no getting around his grimness.

Geveret, he mutters. This is no place for a lady.

33.

The Georgian woman and I are on the balcony when a swallowtail butterfly rises from the bed of lupines in the garden below and flutters onto the back of my hand. Black with blue panes like bits of stained glass lodged in its wings. We stand in the sunshine, breathing in the perfumed air, listening to the distant call of the muezzin. The cyclamen are in bloom. They cover the eastern perimeter of the garden dappled in shade. A pink-and-white carpet of cyclamen. I shake my hand to free the butterfly, but it clings to my knuckle, like a lover, a nettle. The Georgian woman rustles with excitement and points at the sky. She takes a pen and small notepad from her pocket and draws an angel.

Malach, angel, for you, for you he comes, she says in her faltering Hebrew.

34.

Two years before I met you, Rothman and I moved into the apartment on the Street of Shoes. Even in '49, when the country was barely older than a newborn, the central bus station thrummed with energy. From a small tool shop nearby, the music of Laila Mourad, the Egyptian actress and singer who began her life as a Jew and converted to Islam so she could remain a film star, swelled through the neighborhood. The smell of leather and glue drifted up from Baruch's shoe factory, where I worked with a dozen girls like me. All of us from somewhere else, listening to Laila Mourad, a woman forced to prove she was no longer a Jew again and again. Like her, we wore the mask of belonging until we fit into it.

One morning I was on the balcony, drinking

coffee and reading the newspaper *Davar* for Hebrew beginners, when a car horn blared. I heard my name shouted above the din. It was Rothman.

Come on, he said.

I leaned over the railing, my heart in my mouth. Where to?

He'd been gone twenty-six days. It was the longest we'd ever been apart since the war, since Siberia.

Beit HaHayal, he said.

And why would I want to go to a veterans' facility? I said, trying and failing to curb my petulance, my anger, my pleasure. Around Rothman, I was always trying to contain myself.

To keep me company. I've got a delivery.

Give me a minute, I said, and rushed inside to dress.

Rothman was twenty-two, still a soldier in the army. I was eighteen. We lived together like brother and sister. A year later, he'd introduce us, Max. He'd say to me, I've met your perfect someone. Rothman deeded the apartment to us as a wedding gift. He said he owed me his life when, in fact, I owed him mine. It was a gift I didn't want, an apartment saturated with his presence. Every room was Rothman, but you agreed to take it. That was our first mistake. We should have bounded for Jerusalem, or Beersheba, or left the country. We should have run somewhere far from him.

He drove an army-issued white Peugeot. Rothman navigated the military the way he navigated the camp. He scrounged, he stole, he lied, he procured, he knew instinctively what his superiors wanted and gave it to them. He knew what I wanted but never gave it to me.

It was October, and we basked in the dregs of summer. The sun was bright and caught on the twisted limbs of the ficus trees that lined the boulevards. I canted my head out the window as we drove through the city toward the Yarkon River. We passed Sheikh Munis, an abandoned Arab village inhabited by Jews from Syria and Yemen. We saw Bedouin shepherds grazing their sheep near a supermarket, and the construction site that would one day become Tel Aviv University. We drove to Tel Baruch, the road lined with sabras, the thorny leaves big as plates, and citrus trees heavy with orange and pomelo.

I'm hungry, I said.

I'll feed you when we're finished, Rothman said.

I grumbled but he only grinned and promised to stop at our favorite restaurant on Yehuda Ha Maccabee Street on the way back to our apartment, where we'd feast on shawarma, mujadra, and malabeh, for which the Syrian owner wouldn't charge because every month or so Rothman brought him two dozen cartons of Gitanes that disappeared from a ship's manifest. Rothman spun the radio dial past Radio Lebanon and Radio Cairo, to *Kol Yisrael*, the Voice of Israel. I kept my eyes on the trees and sun-scorched fields rushing past so as not to stare at him. My gaze was like a homing pigeon unable to stop itself from returning to its cote.

We soon entered the gates of Beit HaHayal, once a sanitarium for British soldiers during the First and Second World Wars, and we pulled into a parking spot beside a fig tree, the scent a narcotic for wasps, buzzing and slurping at the nectar before burrowing into the fruit to lay their eggs. Rothman removed a box from the trunk and lifted it onto his shoulders. I noticed the way his uniform stretched across his back and his belt cinched his waist. I noticed everything about Rothman—the way he sat with his legs crossed, spoke with his hands, how he threw his head back and his jugular throbbed when he laughed, how he smoked and drank and ate and swallowed and smelled like cinnamon and treated me like a bratty sister, and how even in his sleep, he opened his arms and made room for me in his bed when I had nightmares.

White impatiens lined the path to the main building. A well-groomed row of yews hugged the walkway. Rothman waited for me to catch up.

It's beautiful here, I said, inhaling the sharp tang of pine trees. The tension in my shoulders subsided.

Don't dawdle, he said. This is heavy.

The lobby was cool and clean with a gold-and-white mosaic-tiled floor. We went to the front desk, where a middle-aged man wearing a *kippah* greeted us in Hebrew, then Russian. I had deliberately forgotten the Russian I'd learned in the camp; Rothman spoke it fluently. To everyone, he was whatever they wanted him to be. But with me, he was selfish, a tyrant, a savior, a fallen saint, a friend, a brother, a man who disappeared for weeks without word.

Take a walk, he said. I'll be a while.

I resented his commanding tone. Where are you going?

Swim meet.

What?

He shot me an exasperated look. Just go, he said, and pointed toward the French doors that led to the grounds at the back of the facility.

I didn't want to argue, not then, not after being

without him so long.

There was an Olympic-size pool— the water a deep azure. Across the lawn, palm trees and casuarina offered shade. A few families sat at wooden picnic tables, their voices catching on the breeze. I climbed to the small park at the top of the grassy knoll; I hadn't been on a swing since the camp. Each year Rothman had built one from a plank of wood and some rope, which he tied to a tree limb. We enjoyed it all summer, flew like the blue herons on the lake, necks stretched, chests wide, legs pumping.

Beside the pool, a group of young veterans gathered. An instructor with a whistle around his neck and a clipboard in his hands joined them. They greeted each other with quick hugs and slaps on the back. They looked like gods cast in sunshine. A breeze tugged at my dress, and with it, my anger at Rothman dissolved. I didn't want to consider why he had avoided me all month. I didn't want to remember the argument we'd had the night before he'd walked out and left me alone in our apartment on the Street of Shoes. I had drunk too much wine and begged him to dance and rubbed my body against his, and when I lifted my face to be kissed, he turned away to light a cigarette.

You too? He scoffed at me.

What? I said, and held his hand to my cheek. He pinched me hard. My eyes teared, but I didn't cry.

Everybody wants something from me, he'd said, and then cradled my face.

Even when he hurt me, I felt precious to him. I love you, I told him.

I love you too. He sighed.

Then let's . . . I kissed his jaw, his eyelids, and tasted the bitter sweat in the crease of his neck. His pulse a heavy thud under my lips.

He slipped a hand between my legs. Like this?

He wanted, I think, to shock me, but I had convinced myself long ago that if there was ever a chance for us to become lovers, I would take it.

Embarrassed, I hid my face in his collar and said, Yes.

Come, he led me into the bedroom, and when we got there, he sat on the bed and put the cigarette out on the bottom of his boot and said, Strip.

I took off my clothes and waited, eyes shut, bracing for rejection. I was young. I had no idea what he would think of my body, what anyone would think of it. Back then I was skinny, small with lonely hips and large mournful breasts.

Are you sure? Rothman said.

I nodded. My throat tight, I couldn't squeeze out a word. He was gentle as I knew he would be, but even I, a complete novice, could tell there was something wrong. He made no attempt at romance and there was little passion, only a sad mechanical execution. The whole business lasted maybe ten minutes. He barely let me touch him. I don't think Rothman particularly likes being touched, not in that way, at least not by women, though he has pretended otherwise when it suited him, when he needed a wife to keep up appearances and to help entertain business associates. It never took long for his wives to realize that his passionate nature didn't necessarily extend into the bedroom. I should have understood, but I was too naive then and Rothman had tried his best to protect me from that part of his life. In the camp he made sure I was never alone, but always in the company of the children and matrons. It makes me wonder what he must have endured with the guards and the other inmates who'd created a crude system of reward and punishment. I remember after the war there were towns we were forced to leave in a hurry.

As we lay breathing in the warm evening air, I sensed his unease and thought to comfort him in case he regretted what we'd just done.

We're perfect for each other, I said, threading my hand through his. You're perfect. I kissed his shoulder.

What the fuck are you talking about? Scowling, he bolted upright.

He was really angry, which made me so nervous, I stuttered, something I hadn't done since I was a little girl.

I, I just meant, we're good together. I placed my palm on his back. You and me like this, lovers and friends, family, I said. You're my family. Nothing could be more perfect than being with you forever.

I had loved him for so long, I didn't know anything else. No one I met came close to Rothman. I hugged him and whispered, My love, marry me, certain that would cure the sudden awkwardness that had sprung between us. I was sure that what we'd done was proof that he loved me the way I loved him, but he said nothing. He stood up. I blushed, noticing that he hadn't even bothered to remove his trousers.

He straightened his uniform. I have to get back to the base, he said, and left eighty lira on the nightstand.

To this day, I don't know if he meant for me to

feel cheap or if it was a way for him to underscore the transactional nature of all of his relationships.

On the swing in Beit HaHayal, I pumped my legs and swung so high, my body was no more than light and dust and air. Pine needles fell to the ground. My sandals slipped off my feet, and my heels scraped the dirt, raising clouds of dust. I heard the men near the pool laughing. The swim instructor blew his whistle. They undressed, talking animatedly, unbuttoning their shirts, revealing ropey necks and muscled chests. They truly were like gods. I searched for Rothman and found him among those men. He glanced up the hill, and I waved. His face was stony and resolute. The men unzipped their pants and then it seemed that everything slowed. There was the hollow snap of wood, the grind and click of metal, the sounds of prosthetic limbs being shed. There were men without legs who held on to men without arms. Rothman lifted his chin, defiant, daring me to look away as he stripped out of his clothes. I saw the deep, ugly, twisted flesh that bisected his right thigh as clear as if I were standing beside him. I recalled those many nightmarish weeks in Kolyma, his high fever, his bottomless screams, and when the camp doctor wanted to amputate, Rothman begged, *Kill me.* Even then he wouldn't allow me to see the damage. He'd kept the wound and later the scar concealed from me. I thought it was out of love and Rothman's innate vanity. I put it from my mind, knowing how upset it would make him if I ever alluded to or remarked on his injury. We had been together so long that I barely noticed the slight limp he worked so hard to conceal. It was as much a part of him as his laughter or his wit. I think he viewed that imperfection as a mortal weakness, especially in front of me, the girl who loved him, worshipped him. It was all right for others to appear that way; he even preferred it. It gave him leverage, but he couldn't abide it in himself. Except now it seemed he had found his brothers-in-arms, men just as virile and even more damaged than him. They didn't view him as weak. He was one of them, a broken god.

The men hobbled to the edge of the pool, the instructor counted to three, and they tipped their bodies into the water and sank. I held my breath. The instructor called out and they bobbed to the surface like corks and swam gracefully and unhindered, propelling themselves forward. I stared blindly at the trees that fenced in the grounds, clutching the folds of my dress, whispering Rothman, Rothman.

My voice booming louder, Rothman, but he couldn't hear me, and even if he had, I knew he wouldn't answer.

35.

Weeks later, I ask Dr. S, How long have I been here?

The doctor mumbles something I can't make out.

It's a late afternoon appointment, different from our 10:00 a.m. meetings. No tea, no wafers, all business. He examines the contents of his tobacco pouch, frowning, sinks his meerschaum pipe with the wolf carving in and gently lifts one corner, fills the bowl, then uses his thumb to pack more leaves in.

I've told you not to concern yourself with time.

He strikes a match, then draws hard on the pipe and follows it up with two rapid puffs, producing a cloud of cherries.

But I'm well now. I want to leave, I say.

Where will you go?

Dr. S seems more stooped today than yesterday. There's a tremor in his hand as he drops the match into the ashtray. His tie is askew, and his socks are mismatched—one navy, the other black. An easy mistake if he were dressing in the dark, taking care not to wake his young wife, but the woman's picture is still missing from the desk. What conclusion can I come to but that she's left him.

Home, I say. May I? And point to the lopsided cigarette box one of his children or grandchildren made for him. He slides it from one corner of the desk to the other like a toy train car. For a moment, he seems to ignore my request. I sigh and think that I'll just have to wait until I get back to my room, where I've hidden the carton of Dunhill that Rothman brought me. It arrived on a shipment from London via Delhi, but I prefer to keep those cigarettes for when I'm alone writing to you or making paper boats. I've gotten very good at making them. I string the boats together into a chain. My mother used to make them from old newspaper when I was a girl, and we'd sail them on the lake in summer. The trick was to see how long it would take for them to capsize. Sometimes we'd see Tomasz and his father, the town plumber, there. Tomasz made his boats out of tree bark and poplar leaves. They were a natural wonder and always managed to bobble along while our paper ones sank.

I enjoy *schnorring* cigarettes from Dr. S, who in his own way is like a plumber, a Roto- Rooter man of the mind. Through the open window I can hear the children behind the stucco wall. Is it an orphanage? I ask.

What? His brow beetles as he jams a file into a drawer.

I point out the window toward the *Collège des Frères*. Is it an orphanage or just a school? Do the children live there year-round?

It's a boarding school.

What's the difference? I puff on the cigarette.

Parents who love them, he says.

I turn his words over in my mind. The strains of the Chopin nocturne meander through the hall. I close my eyes, almost giddy to hear Tomasz-Henrik play again, each note whispering Rivkaleh.

36.

My mother loved me best at the beginning of the war—love driven by worry and sacrifice. Harder when worry falls off and indifference sets in. No one except generals and profit mongers imagines a war will last years. Days, weeks, a month or two, but never years, though history is full of wars that have lasted decades. By the end, my mother, like the rest of the camp, was infiltrated, outflanked by disease brought on by overexertion, hunger, and cold. But in that first year when we ran in the fields and made daisy-chain crowns in summer and the snow fell like tatted lace in the fall and lashed at us through the long winter, she was ferocious in her love, certain it would keep me alive.

I don't think I ever told you about the man who caught me staring through Lenya's window. She was one of four prostitutes in bunk eight. He came up behind me and in minutes he had torn my woolen stockings and told me that, if I made a sound, the guards would shoot me, and he pointed to the watchtower, where two men held Kalashnikovs and passed a flask between them. I should have known they had no bullets. We barely had food, except what we could grow in the short summer season and early fall. The ammunition was sent to the soldiers on the front, where Papa was. The man was skin and bones, still I thought he'd crush me. I must have screamed. My mother was bringing clean sheets to the barrack matrons and heard me. She came running, bearing the thick paddle she used to stir the laundry in those great steel tubs. I don't remember how many times she hit him; he fell without a sound. Fifty years later and I can still smell his rotten breath and see the dark yellow stains on his *gatkes*, that long underwear the men in the camp wore and rarely took off, if they were lucky enough to have a pair.

The story around the camp was that he was drunk and fell and hit his head. Only Lenya knew the truth. She saw it all through her window and spat on the dead man. I don't know what my mother said to keep her quiet, but Lenya's clothes were always clean and her bedding the first to be dried. When my mother was dying, Lenya stayed with her, and when she was dead, Lenya was the one who gave me the news, *Du nebech meydl*, You poor girl; she caressed my cheek, *Deyn mameh ist toyt*, Your mother is dead, and pulled me into her arms. My face buried in the sharp angles of her breasts. Rothman made sure we said *kaddish* for Mama. Two of the other prisoners buried her in the forest. Lenya paid an inmate to inscribe a stone. We placed it on her grave. Maybe it's still there.

37.

The Georgian woman enters without knocking. Rothman has given her a small gift. She shows me the bottle of Trésor perfume, still in its box. He's asked her to deliver another sales contract.

Thank you, I say, placing the envelope on the desk. I mime, You smell nice.

She beams at me, her gold teeth sparkling.

When she leaves, I open the envelope and make a long chain of paper boats.

After midnight I sneak into Tomasz-Henrik's room and find him waiting for me, an eager swain. We greet each other with chaste kisses. He feeds me the orange he's saved from lunch. I give him the chain of boats as a gift. He tells me they are beautiful. He tells me I am beautiful and sighs in my ear, Rivkaleh, *mayn ketzeleh,* my kitten.

38.

I pay the cabdriver for the ride from Ben Gurion Airport to Tel Aviv and walk into the entrance of our old building on the Street of Shoes. It no longer smells of *tzimmis* and stuffed cabbage, but of fried fish and roast pork. Three flights up, I'm puffed out and lean against the jamb and insert the key I've carried on a chain for four decades. After a brief and intense struggle, the chamber in the lock releases and the door swings open. How small the flat is compared to our apartment on West End Avenue. The first thing I do is switch on all the lights. They flicker as if waking from a deep sleep and then beam steadily. Rothman made sure the electricity worked, and he put in new bulbs. The living room is a narrow rectangle, the kitchen a square. More than forty winters have abused the window casements. The plaster has peeled to expose the rebar, and there are islands of black mold on the ceiling. Years of dust and soot are on the floor. A graveyard of insects litter the kitchen counter. The furniture is still covered in the sheets we draped them in. We hadn't expected to stay away so long. The sheets are stained with mold and eaten through by bed worms. The mustiness makes me cough; my eyes tear and my throat is scratchy. It's cold but I open the windows and they gasp and tremble as I do with the effort. The night sky presses against the balcony, and the lights of Tel Aviv pulse to a rhythm I no longer know.

I tear the ragged sheets off the bed. They practically disintegrate in my hands. I switch on the *dood*, unsure whether the hot water heater still works, relieved at the familiar whoosh of the pilot catching, relieved that Rothman sent a man to take care of the plumbing and install a new stove and refrigerator.

If you'd given me more time, I could've gotten the place painted and professionally cleaned before you arrived. Now it'll have to be done while you're there, he said. Meanwhile, he had a phone installed, something that would have taken months without his connections.

It takes time for the water to heat, so I light a

cigarette, wrap my arms around myself, and trudge into the master bedroom. Outside, someone shouts in a language I've never heard. Days from now when I meet the woman next door, I learn it's Tagalog. She is a caretaker from the Philippines, caring for an old survivor who lost his wife and children in Majdanek. It's all he ever talks about, she grumbles. It's all she ever talks about too, as if in caring for him she's absorbed every memory the old man ever had. A Vespa sputters past the building. An airplane flies too low, making the windows rattle, but all I hear and see are the crowded images of us before the fall, or the end, or whatever it is we called the devastation that tore us from here.

Because I can think of nothing else, because all at once I'm frightened of being alone in the apartment, I rush to the kitchen sink and run the tap. After a series of fits and starts, the water gushes from the spout. I drink palmfuls that taste of rust and imagine the water being dredged up from the bottom of an ancient cistern. The refrigerator stands like a sentry on watch. I wipe a hand across my mouth and peer into the empty murk, then plug the appliance into the wall socket. A quick spark, a hum, and the apartment is alive again. Thank God for Rothman. Out on the balcony it's easy to see where the Street of Shoes dips into the old central bus station. They've dismantled it and built a new station nearby, far uglier than the old one. Still, the immigrants have remained, mostly Africans and Asians now, living in a grimier swelter of poverty and stink than we did.

The temperature is warmer outside than it is in. I remember the evenings we ate our dinner on the balcony and watched buses come and go, passengers waiting, bundles at their feet, chickens in wire cages to be slaughtered for the Shabbos meal. There was an old bearded Jew who lived in the station, beseeching men to don *tefillin* so *moshiach,* the anointed one, the great messiah would come. From our perch we saw the filthy, beating heart of the city, where the sacred and the profane collided. Now all I see is the light at the brothel, if it is a brothel, blinking its cold blue eye.

When the water is hot, I undress, toes cringing against the cold tile. I wash off the flight. I wash off the Belgian, I wash off forty years and am born anew, again. A cockroach scuttles near the drain. The creature makes a valiant run for it, but in the end is swept into the current. Wrapped in my coat, I climb into bed and hang on as if shipwrecked.

* * *

Our first year of marriage. The hours it took us to unwind after a performance. We stayed up until three or four in the morning, until sunlight clawed at the horizon. The central bus station was deserted and the neighborhood so noisy during the day was silent, muffled as if someone had thrown a blanket over it. In summer no matter how tired we were, the heat made it impossible to sleep. We drank Goldstar beer and smoked packs of whatever Rothman smuggled in, and when we couldn't get the European brands, we bought the cheapest Israeli cigarettes, Nelson's and Noblesse, picking twigs out with our fingertips, watching them catch fire when we couldn't reach them. We listened to American jazz and ate thick wedges of watermelon and munched on roasted peanuts and sunflower seeds. The night sky was dark with only a star or two pinned to it. Everything we said, no matter how inane, seemed important and tenuous as if the world were cradling us in its silken web. We heard old Shalom (Remember him?), our neighbor on the floor below, snoring, and joked about how if he snored any louder, he'd strip the paint off the cars. If he snored any louder, the streetlamps would explode. If he snored any louder, he'd cause a tidal wave. We carried on like that, laughing so hard, beer spit out of our noses, until I blurted, if he snored any louder, fruit would drop from the trees. The most innocuous statement of the evening and yet you turned pale and quiet, retreating into yourself.

What's wrong? I said, hoping to draw you back to me.

The trees.

What about them?

Nothing.

Tell me.

In the camp.

Yes?

My head's spinning, you said.

It's the heat. I poured you a glass of water.

We fell silent, lying side by side on a thin foam mattress we'd dragged onto the balcony earlier that night. I was aware of your body, of its heat, each pore a tiny furnace. I thought of how all the parts of you fit all the parts of me, how even my tongue had found a home in your mouth. My heart in your heart. I wanted to make love and fretted that I wanted it more than you did. While you searched for the right words, I tried to remember the last time we had sex. Was it that morning? The night before? Days ago? What if time had slipped like a chain on a gear and I had no recollection, no way of trusting the day, the hour, or what I knew?

What happened to the trees? I said, picturing us making love right there, out in the open on our little balcony, aroused at the thought of who might hear us or see us, which neighbors would look, which would turn away, who would listen? How quick we would have to be, how slow and quiet?

It's not about the trees. It's the woman, you said, exasperated, as if I should have known who she was.

A grand lady, a duchess, in a blue riding habit. She rode her horse outside Bergen-Belsen all spring and summer. She dressed him in indigo plumes. Her footman wore a royal blue uniform. He accompanied her everywhere.

She must have been married to one of the officers, I said.

Probably.

What kind of trees were they?

The lights were out in the building across from us. Everyone was asleep. It was very late and I knew it would be dawn soon. The drivers would return, and the street would rumble with bus engines.

Cherry trees, you said.

Cherries, I repeated. What did she do?

It's not what she did. You stubbed out the

cigarette you'd just lit.

I picked it out of the ashtray, an old habit, to save for later.

You turned on your side away from me. Your voice dropped. I had to strain to hear you say, She picked the fruit off the trees. We weren't allowed to touch them. We watched her gorging on cherries while we starved for them, for her. When had any of us seen a woman like that?

Your breath deepened and you finally turned to face me and kissed my neck. Relieved, I loosened the drawstring on your shorts. You slipped the straps of my camisole down over my shoulders.

We were invisible, you muttered. Garbage to her. She knew what that place was, what would become of us.

You slipped your hands under my hips.

Was that all? I said, and wrapped my legs around your waist.

She tortured us.

How?

She threw handfuls of cherries over the fence and watched us drop to our knees and dig for them like dogs in the dirt, stuffing them into our mouths soil and all until the guard cocked his rifle and asked us if we wanted to die that day. We'd have gladly died for the chance to get our hands around her skinny white neck.

Show me, I said.

You placed your palms on either side of my face and kissed me. We fucked.

Old Shalom's snores rumbled through the night. A breeze blew, carrying the smell of the distant sea.

You held me in your arms and said, What a play she would make.

Maybe you're mistaken. Maybe all she wanted was to feed you, I said. Maybe she was just trying to be kind.

But you had already fallen asleep, and the next day we awoke to the news that there had been an attack on the Burma Road near the Nachshon Junction. Three soldiers killed. Old Shalom knocked on our door. We had no telephone then and used the one in Baruch's shoe factory, where old Shalom was the manager. He gave you the message that you were called into the reserves and were to report that afternoon to your unit commander at the Tel HaShomer military base. We never imagined you'd be gone two months.

39.

Dr. S coughs into a large white handkerchief. He sets his vacant stare out the window, tapping his long fingers on the green blotter.

Are you all right? I ask.

Fine, he snaps.

You don't look it.

He brushes away my concern. Tell me about Rothman. Is he the reason you returned to Israel?

No, I say, and blush.

But he's someone to you, someone special, he prods.

Yes.

Dr. S coughs so hard, I can hear his bones grind against each other. When had he gotten so thin?

Let's call for tea, I say. I can use a cup.

No more distractions, he warns.

Sister Francoise, I call, knowing she is hovering outside the door. The doctor isn't feeling well.

Dr. S gives me a baleful look.

Sister Francoise strides in, frowning. She takes Dr. S's pulse, places a hand on his forehead.

It's nothing, he says. A seasonal cold.

In a stern voice, she says, Are you trying to make yourself sick? You belong in bed, not infecting everyone with your germs.

Then Sister Francoise gives me a kind look and says, Come, my dear, I'll take you back to your room, then we'll see about putting the doctor to bed.

40.

You left to join your unit. I spent the days rehearsing *Medea* and came home late at night to an empty apartment. The loneliness was claustrophobic and made worse by the grim news in the papers. Rothman came around every few days to see that I was all right and to store the more expensive contraband he dealt in, in the spare bedroom. We'd walk on the beach, get something to eat at one of the cafés. He helped pass the time and I was grateful for his company, but then he'd leave again, and I'd sink into a well I couldn't climb out of. I smoked too much, forgot to eat, and drank more than I should have. I thought about Medea a lot, about Jason, and her children, about how easy it was to lose love, to lose everything that grounded you and then have that ground give way, spinning you out into the *nischt ahin, nischt aher*, where nothing mattered or existed, where you were swallowed by time and haunted by memory.

You'd been gone five weeks. I was in dress rehearsals. It was midnight. I'd just gotten home and made myself comfortable with a whiskey on the balcony. The heat of the liquor made me break into a sweat. Someone was playing the oud, a melody that wove like a gold thread through the streets. There was a knock on the door. My stomach lurched into my throat. I imagined the worst as I often do. I imagined a soldier in dress uniform, a messenger behind that door ready to give me the news that you were wounded or dead. I imagined you standing there waiting for me to answer because you'd forgotten your key or were afraid I wouldn't be there. My heart thumped so hard, I felt faint. When I flung the door open, I saw Rothman. His face unrecognizable, beaten, bleeding, one eye swollen shut, his bottom lip split. I half carried him in. I thought it might have been a car accident and asked if he wanted me to take him to a hospital.

He pleaded with me not to.

His clothes were filthy, and I helped him undress. I switched on the *dood*, so there'd be enough hot water for him. He could barely stand in the shower.

I washed him the way I would a child. Dark bruises bloomed on his ribs, back, and buttocks. He'd been kicked over and over again. We managed to stop the nosebleed, but then my breath shuddered at the trail of blood that trickled between his legs. He groaned in pain. His bad leg shook, and I was afraid he'd fall. I toweled him dry as gently as I could and gave him a few pain pills I had stashed. Rothman took the pills and asked that I stay with him. I lay beside him in the bed, scared to leave him alone, worried his ribs were broken, that he'd punctured a lung, that he'd run a fever.

It was dark. I couldn't see him but felt him trembling.

Who did this to you? I whispered. I couldn't imagine one person doing this kind of damage and asked, How many were there?

He remained silent.

It's all right, I said, and wrapped him in my arms, taking care not to hurt him.

At some point during the night he said, Three. They knew me from the beach.

There was something in his voice that I'd never heard before—despair and something much worse, a brokenness. I don't know how to explain what I felt except that I was frightened for him and yet I was never stronger. Rothman needed me. It was the first time I saw him cry, not just a tear he'd quickly swipe at the thought of the sister and parents he'd lost, but a real sob scraped up from some charred place Rothman had never acknowledged. I thought of what my father said about how we are all vessels and that our souls are the light inside them that shatter into the darkness. It wasn't fear that made Rothman cry, because he's fearless; it was shame. We never spoke about what those men did to him or what they took from him.

He stayed with me a week. We didn't talk much but he did ask if I'd heard from you. My answer was always the same—no. I went to rehearsal and came home to find Rothman smoking on the balcony, staring out at the rooftops. The world far from him and he from it.

The last night we went to bed, he turned to me, his lips no longer swollen, a jaundiced bruise on his jaw. The black and blue around his eyes beginning to fade. I had never felt so close to him and had never seen him so vulnerable. I caressed his cheek, and he kissed the palm of my hand, and we made love in a way that I had always imagined we would. We comforted each other. We knew each other and shared a deep intimacy. It was never a rejection of you, Max. He was gone the next morning and I wouldn't see him for months afterward. You returned some weeks later and I found that I was pregnant. I had no words for the joy I felt. Rothman didn't know, at least not then. You were my husband, and that meant Asher was yours in all the ways that mattered.

41.

Dr. S is on medical leave. Dr. E is his replacement, a middle-aged woman in gold wire-framed glasses that give her the appearance of a big-eyed bug. There's a photograph of such an insect in a volume on entomology titled *Insects of the Holy Land* on a shelf in the sunroom opposite the piano Tomasz-Henrik plays. Her frosted hair is the same length as mine. I think the Sisters must have gotten to her too. We're twins sitting in silence, our hands cupped in our laps like schoolgirls reprimanded for smoking in the bathroom. I am angry with Dr. S for leaving without saying goodbye. Bereft. How dare he!

When the hour is up, she opens the door and waits for the orderly on call to take me to my room. I search for the vodka the Georgian woman bought with the money Rothman gave me. But it isn't in my shoe, or coat pocket, nor the desk drawer where these pages are. I keep meaning to send these letters to you, Max, but there's always so much more to say. The last place I search, and by this time I'm exhausted, is the narrow cleft between the bed and the wall. There like a treasure in Ali Baba's cave, the bottle is inside a stocking, hanging from the iron bed frame. I take a *shluk* and then another and another and the vodka burns through the rage and the sorrow, but it doesn't quite reach the frozen earth beneath.

The next time Dr. E and I meet, I gather my courage and say, I want to go home.

Of course you do, she says, it's only natural. Her voice carries just the right amount of sympathy for me to feel hopeful.

Dr. E, I say, Dr S's release forms are in the middle drawer of his desk. All you need is to sign them, and I can leave.

I understand, she says. You must be homesick. You miss your life. You miss your husband.

Yes, I say. Yes.

I wait for her to reach into the drawer, but instead, she looks out the window at the crows thrashing the air; their violence is mesmerizing.

In some cultures, crows are harbingers of death, she says, while in others they represent spiritual transformation. We aim for something like that here. An emotional transformation. Our goal is to help you create a bridge toward the center, toward equilibrium. From what I've read in your file, you haven't found that center yet.

I want a cigarette, but Dr. E doesn't smoke, and Dr. S's cigarette box has vanished like Dr. S himself.

She places a hand on my shoulder. It's surprisingly heavy and damp. Let me help you get there.

The overhead light snags on her glasses, and I see my reflection in them. She runs her palm over my head like the Queen of Razor Blades, her hand sliding across the slick plane of my scalp.

People have a tendency to live in the past, Dr. E says. They prefer memory to reality.

My eyes slip past her face to the photograph on her desk of an old woman.

Is that your mother?

Dr. E is surprised by the question, but then her face softens, and she says, Yes it is.

When is Dr. S coming back?

I don't know. He's on extended medical leave. She looks at the clock on the wall.

Is he sick?

She smiles benignly and says, Time's up, my dear. I'll see you tomorrow.

Sister Francoise appears at the door to escort me to my room.

Max, maybe if you call Dr. E on the telephone, she'll listen to you. Tell her I'm fine, fully recovered. The small matter of the nervous exhaustion that brought me here is resolved. You're an impressive man. People take you seriously. When you speak, they listen. Tell her to send me home. You don't know what it's like to be in this room. Each day it grows smaller and the bed narrower. A steady erasure. Make the call, Max. Please.

42.

A few weeks in our old apartment on the Street of Shoes, and a routine emerges. Each morning I wake to the roar of buses, car horns, and the modulated chirping of sparrows that perch for long minutes on the balcony before swooping off. After a leisurely breakfast, I head to the *makolet* to buy fresh rolls and cheese for lunch. On the way, I pass a group of African women sitting cross-legged on straw mats, selling fruit and vegetables. They wear peacoats, and bright kerchiefs round their heads, their feet in open-toed slippers. The December cold bores into the bones, so I bring them socks. They give me a sack of oranges. Between the shoppers, the *sheyroot* vans that transport passengers from city to city, taxis, trades people shouting, and the brisk business in the nearby souk, the decibel level in the old central bus station is as deafening as ever.

Today when I reach the stuccoed bungalow with the blue light, I stop at the sight of the young woman with the bleached hair and large green eyes. Her cheeks are drawn and pitted with scars of teenage acne. She sits in a moldering armchair, pale with fatigue, smoking a cigarette, absently rocking a baby carriage with her foot. I cannot see the child. Usually, the boy sits up and plays with the plastic rings on his carriage, mouth slack and drooling. His clothes are either too big or too small, hand-me-downs from some charity or another.

May I see your baby, I say in Hebrew.

Yeled yoshen, she says in a thick Russian accent; the boy is sleeping. She looks at me with suspicion and grinds the cigarette under her heel.

I'll be careful, I say.

The boy, possibly a year or more, is too large for the small carriage. He lies on his back, legs dangling over the sides. He isn't sleeping. He's gazing at the ceiling, until I come into his line of vision. Then he stretches his small hand toward me, and I place my forefinger in the center of his palm, shivering at the urgency with which he grips it.

You from government? the girl says.

No. I live in the neighborhood. I bow low and coo at the boy.

Around here? You?

Yes. Can I give him a cookie?

I had put a package of petite-beurre biscuits in my bag for him before I left the apartment, hoping he'd be out today. Her eyes travel the length of me, calculating the cost of my shoes, wool coat, and leather handbag. She's about to answer when a car screeches to a stop and honks its horn. The baby startles. He lets go of my finger and wails. *Nebach*, such big tears. I want so much to hold him in my arms but am afraid his mother will get angry. Brushing me aside, she scoops him up and rushes to the car, whose back end is smashed, the trunk held shut with a rope. She leans in through the window, the child balanced on her hip, and kisses the driver full on the mouth. His hands stretch round and squeeze her rump like it's a melon. He's got a boxer's nose, broken more than once, pounded flat at the bridge, round as a tulip bulb at the tip. He's about forty and bald, and right away I don't like him. She slaps his hand and kisses him again. Mouths parted, they draw in each other's breath. I'm pinned to the spot by the image of them, a family on the curb of that dirty street, a family where garbage collects and streaks of bat guano decorate the top floors of the buildings.

He points in my direction and says in Russian, Who's she? one of the few phrases I still remember in that language. The girl says something quick and sharp that I can't make out and the man gives me a menacing look and glares at me with suspicion. The baby whimpers and the driver steps out of the car. He lifts the boy in his arms, sails him into the air again and again, each time higher, and the child, flaying his arms, doesn't know whether to laugh or cry. He's too young to be trapped between this kind of terror and pleasure. I want to shout at the man to leave the baby alone. I want to pluck the child out of the air and take him home with me. A minute later he deposits the boy into his mother's arms, gives her another squeeze, and sinks a few shekels into her front pocket before driving away.

You still here? the mother says to me, and plops the boy down in the carriage.

I give him my hand again and he latches on to it, gazing at me with his large brown eyes, and I have to bite my lip to keep it from trembling. I ask the woman if I can hold the baby.

How much you pay? she says.

What? I recoil.

How much? Every day I see you walk here. You look at baby. Today you want hold him. What you want tomorrow?

Nothing. I grip my bag with both hands, all of me cringing, flushed with shame. Sorry to bother you, I bob my head in apology, in subservience. I am groveling. I've made a terrible mistake.

Don't go, she says. He very beautiful, yes? How much you give to hold him?

My heart beats fast. I take a good look at the peeling stucco on the bungalow, the front door half opened. I can see inside to the sofa, where two women sit, one African, the other white like this woman, whose age is impossible to tell. She could be eighteen or thirty. An Israeli game show is on the TV. The host has a deep tan and he keeps shouting the word *rabotai* when he wants the audience's attention. Mizrahi music drifts in from the souk nearby, and cars speed down the road. I notice the young mother's hands—the chipped nails, the torn cuticles, the skin red and cracked around the knuckles. Rough working hands. Familiar hands.

Five shekels, I say.

Ten, she says.

I give her the money and watch it disappear into the same pocket the driver stuffed the cash into.

The baby is blond. His hair is shellacked to his forehead, and when I lift him up, a fetid stench rises from his diaper and I'm right back in the children's home in Siberia. Only this time the noise falls away and something like peace fills me. He looks at me and grins, a delightful toothy grin, and my heart clenches in quiet agony. His diaper is wet and heavy with shit. He stinks.

I can change him for you, I say. An angry rash creeps down his legs.

Diapers finished. Too much money. She says this almost coyly.

What part of Russia are you from? I say.

Why? She frowns.

If you want, I'll bring diapers for him.

Maybe you bring milk too?

All right, milk too.

And cigarettes. Her eyes strip my face. She sees straight to the heart of my longing.

What you doing in this part of town, old woman? You from church, or synagogue?

I told you I live down the street.

So what you want? She pokes the air with her bony finger.

Your boy needs a clean diaper. He could get an infection.

He need milk. Nothing left here, she says, and grabs hold of her flat breasts. She slumps back in the chair.

It's hard to imagine her nursing. The boy whimpers. I nuzzle his neck, sour with sweat. What's his name?

Leon. Everybody love Leon. Except he's pain in ass. Don't let me sleep. I work night in hotel cleaning. Leon always hungry. Always crying.

How old is he?

She squints and tugs another cigarette out from under the seat cushion. Maybe fifteen months. You got match?

I shake my head.

She bends down and reaches for a box under the chair.

He's small for fifteen months.

What you want from me, lady?

I'll bring you the diapers and the milk, if you let me look after him sometimes. Free babysitting. You can sleep all day if you want. I'm free all the time. Think about it. Leon rests his head on my shoulder. See, he likes me already.

She puckers her lips and picks at a cuticle. Why you do this?

He's a sweet boy. I know how hard it is for a

working mother.

You give money, I get what Leon need, she says.

No, I'll bring the groceries.

I kiss Leon on the cheek and lay him in the carriage. He stares at the ceiling and I follow his gaze to the carpet of moths clinging to the stucco and tell myself to walk away and never return. Tell myself I can't help this child or any child. That being with him will not bring Asher back. But my heart, that stubborn beast, refuses to listen. I rationalized that if I could just care for baby Leon, then it would make up for all the *kinder* in the camp who I didn't take care of. All the babies who cried through the night, the ones I ignored, the ones I sent back to their beds. If I could do this for Leon, then it would be as if I'd saved them, as if I'd saved Asher.

Forty minutes later, I return with the diapers and a quart of milk. The mother and the baby are gone. I leave the shopping bag near the closed door, angry that it took so long. Angry the boy is inside, where I cannot reach him.

43.

Max, I don't want to trouble you, but I need you to contact Dr. E. Rothman says it's a small matter, a phone call, no more. All you have to do is say that I'm needed at home. Rothman will take care of the travel plans. It really is too bad Dr. S is no longer here. I'm sure he was ready to sign my release papers. Sister Francoise hinted as much. She said he'd worked himself into exhaustion and took an extended holiday in Switzerland, a lovely chalet in the Alps. No one knows when he'll return.

Please make the call. I can't think what's keeping you from it. I know you've spoken to Rothman. He's laughingly suggested an escape plan if you don't come through. I assured him you would. Perhaps you're writing again? Your imagination reignited by my absence. I know how single-minded you get when you're working, but there isn't much time. I bet if you came here and insisted on my release, Dr. E wouldn't dare say no. Please come, Max. I don't want to alarm you. It's just that Dr. E is an enthusiastic sort, the kind who in her zeal to do good can be impetuous in her prescriptions. I'm sure she's competent, but there are rumors about therapies and cocktails of medications that are like *shedim*, demons that steal your memories. She's already taken Tomasz-Henrik to the treatment room on the fourth floor. Dr. S called it the room of last resort, but Dr. E sees no reason to wait. Since then, Tomasz-Henrik has not played the nocturne, has not played at all, not a single note. You'd have to know him to understand how unusual this is. Even with his injury, he played. She's done something to him, stolen his music, excised it from him. *What if she does the same to me; what if she takes Asher?* I went to see Tomasz-Henrik in the sunroom this morning. He wasn't at the piano bench but in a chair facing the garden, an afghan thrown over his knees. He looked small, almost diminished, like he'd been squeezed between a pair of iron plates.

I sat beside him, laid my hand on his, and said, *Zent ir gezunt?* Are you feeling well?

He looked at me and said, I know you.

Yes, you do. I'm Rivkaleh.

Rivkaleh's dead. She died in Kutno more than fifty years ago, he said, and then covered his face with his hands.

Sister Francoise accompanied me down the hall, her habit an accordion bellowing around her ankles.

Be happy for him, she said. The therapies have worked. His wife and daughter are taking him home tomorrow.

44.

The young woman's name is Katya. I bring her milk and diapers, bread and cheese. I bring her and Leon to the apartment on the Street of Shoes. I am so excited, I can't feel my feet. My hands tingle. She complains there are too many stairs. Lungs not so good, she says.

Give me Leon, I say, and carry him up, out of breath, my old sagging body straining to climb. My legs are shaking when I reach the door. The child nuzzles my neck, smacking his lips against my ear. Oh, Max, it's heaven.

Before their visit, I scrubbed the place down, aired out the furniture, and filled the refrigerator. I bought sunflowers in the souk and arranged them in a vase I found in one of the kitchen cabinets. I made a thick *krupnik* soup with barley and mushrooms, hoping

Leon would like it. The moment Katya enters, her eyes gleam. She goes from room to room, searching. What's she looking for? She fingers the books on the shelf, the bowl of fruit, smooths the tablecloth with her palm, runs her hands over the curtains, strokes the sofa pillows. A wistful expression on her face. I wonder when she was last in a proper apartment that didn't have bare walls and torn sofas. In the weeks that I've known her and Leon, I never once asked her how long she's been here.

Two years, she sighs. Three in Warsaw.

That's a long time, I say, and think about the toll each year takes, how homesickness is a knife that cuts furrows into the heart.

I show her the master bedroom. She caresses the small bottle of perfume.

Mamushka has one like this, she says, then goes on to the lotions, the loose coins in a dish. Her fingers memorizing as we go.

There's the small bedroom that was mine before Rothman moved out and later became Asher's. Even that room I cleaned, though it took me days to step inside it. His crib is still against the back wall. I almost had Rothman haul it away, but now that Leon is here, I'm glad he didn't. There are toys in the closet and clothes on the top shelf. There's the blue-

and-green sweater I knitted for Asher, the one he wore that winter. I think it just might fit Leon.

You have baby? Katya says, surprise in her voice.

I'll make tea, I say.

She studies the photographs left on the credenza from the old days. Two of Asher, one of us, the three of us together, another of Rothman.

Who these people? she asks.

I tell her.

This man, she points to Rothman, is lover?

No.

He look rich.

He is, I say.

So why not lover?

I set Leon down on a rug in the shape and colors of Planet Earth. I found it in the souk earlier that week and bought it so he wouldn't get a chill playing on the cold tiled floor.

We tried, I say, didn't work.

He don't like woman?

He's been married three times.

Don't mean he like woman.

I guess not, I say, and look at Katya with admiration, though I think her reasoning is too simplistic when it comes to Rothman. There are many ways to love, and he has intimate knowledge of most of them.

This baby, she says, pointing to Asher, who looks directly at the camera, at Rothman, who took the photo, eyes shining, arms outstretched, mouth wide open, three milky teeth gleaming.

He yours?

I nod.

How old he is?

In that picture? About eight months.

Where he is now?

Gone, I say.

What you mean? With husband?

Dead.

The word flies out of my mouth, a winged creature that beats toward heaven. Do you realize the only people I've ever spoken to about Asher are you and Rothman? For years we wiped his name out of our lives, yet he continues to harbor a space without borders. Our boy floats in the blue ether in the world between heaven and earth, waiting to be born again. I run my fingers through Leon's hair and wonder if Asher isn't already here.

Katya looks at her shoes and mumbles, Sorry for baby.

It was a long time ago, I say, and give Leon Asher's wooden dog to play with. He is delighted and gurgles with laughter. The sound is a crystal prism flooding the room with color. I brew tea and put biscuits on a plate with butter and strawberry jam. My heart is so full and I am, dare I say it, Max, happy, *tfoo, tfoo. Kineh horah.*

Katya is bored. She's on the balcony, smoking, squinting into the distance, nervously tapping her foot.

This place is shit hole, she says, and spits onto the pavement below. Marek say we go live in Haifa. Many Russians there. We live next to beach. Leon will like beach.

I'm dismayed by the news. Is Marek the man I saw in the car?

Katya nods, Leon's *papa.*

When do you leave? My stomach cramps, waiting for the answer.

Marek tell me very soon we go.

Oh.

Katya laughs at my expression. He say this for long time already.

She walks back into the living room and picks Leon up. The toy crashes to the floor. His lower lip trembles and he whimpers and grabs hold of Katya's hair in both fists.

Please, you don't need to go yet, I say.

Dark soon. I work in hotel.

Why not leave Leon here? I'll make sure he eats supper, and I can put him to sleep in the crib. I see her turning the idea over in her mind, and I continue. I can give you some money and you can buy Leon a present.

How much money? She bounces him on her hip and kisses his cheek. How much Leon for you to stay with old woman?

Give me a number and we can work something out, I say.

You give—she looks around the room—fifty shekel, but you no put Leon in dead baby's clothes. Okay?

Clothes are too small for him, I whisper.

All right, you nice lady, give forty shekel, she says. You bring him tomorrow one o'clock. I like sleep in morning. Leon knows this, don't you, Leonidik? He look like me, right? She grins.

Just like you, I say, and give her the money, then hold my arms out for Leon, who looks like he's going to cry, sensing his mother is about to leave. Katya sits him on the floor and says, Shalom, Leon. Be good boy for old woman.

45.

I spend the morning watching the children in the *Collège des Frères* play hide and seek. In the camp we played many such games. My favorite was a combination of ring-around-the-rosy and musical chairs. During the summer we played it outside in a field where the grass was high and falling wouldn't hurt. The sun warm and yellow, the sky a blue bowl above our heads. To play, we formed a circle and held each other's hands as tight as we could. Whoever let go first lost. One of the matrons banged a drum and, as time went on, beat it faster than we could keep up with. Rothman was beside me. He never let go. Never. We'd walk round and round until our feet flew out from under us. The smaller children rarely held on for long. They'd land in the grass, dizzy and giggling. When the music came to an abrupt stop, we had to come to a full halt. Sometimes this stopping and starting went on for a long while. More often we'd fall panting and laughing. Rothman holding my hand in his, on our backs we gazed at the clouds that drifted like ships on a sea, wishing they'd take us with them.

46.

The Georgian woman knocks before inserting the key into the lock.

Come, she says, and we walk through the corridor, past the nurses' station, to Dr. E's office. There's a fresh coat of white paint on the walls. Dr. E has insisted on a full renovation, and now the place smells of turpentine.

I take my usual seat across from her.

Today Dr. E wears a grim expression. Her lips form a small O. I'm sorry to be the bearer of bad news, she says.

My heart sinks. What is it?

At first I think something's happened to you, Max, and I can barely catch my breath, and then I think it might be Rothman, and I'm overcome by the strangest sensation, an emptying, as if life were draining out of me.

It's Dr. S, she says. Two days ago, he suffered a cardiac arrest. He died this morning. I thought you'd want to know.

47.

After the first night that I babysit Leon, Katya drops him off in the late afternoons and the next day I return him to her so they can spend a few hours together before she has to leave for work. I meet her roommates, Mila from Ukraine, and Helene from Eritrea. They also work the night shift at the Sheraton Hotel near the beach at Kikar Atarim. There's no one else in the house and I ask Katya, Who took care of Leon before me?

Marek, she says, but now you babysitter, Marek go find job in Haifa.

Leon is delightful. We take long walks. I buy a bigger carriage; I buy him clothes. We stroll down Rothschild Boulevard, where the ficus trees offer shade and stop at the playground. I sit on a bench, content to watch him while he digs in the sandbox. The other women in the park, the nannies, all think he's my grandchild. He looks just like you, they say. I beam at them, but in my heart I imagine he is my child. At night after I bathe him in the kitchen sink and dress him in cotton pajamas that won't irritate his skin, I read to him from the books on Asher's shelf, his small body tucked against mine. In the weeks that I am with him, the rash on his legs disappears. He gains weight. He takes an interest in everything around him. And when he's restless, when I know he's missing Katya, I rock him in my arms and he gazes at me, eyes shining. I believe he loves me.

Rothman calls and says he wants to visit me in the apartment. I tell him that I'm busy.

With what? he asks.

I'm helping a friend, I say.

What friend? I know all of your friends here.

Not this one, I say.

Now you make me curious. I have to come over.

I laugh. I'll let you know when it's convenient.

Is it a lover? I'm jealous.

Goodbye, I say, and hang up, smiling.

48.

My life begins at 4:00 p.m. when Katya leaves for work. On Saturdays when she and Marek take Leon out for the day, I am listless. I miss the boy. When he's not here, I ache for him the way an amputee aches for a phantom limb, just as I did with Asher when he was gone. I cook for Leon, bake for him, cut his hair, sing to him, rub lotion into his baby flesh. My heart is a door that swings open whenever I'm with him. I'm alive again. This is my fate. He's the reason I'm here, to help him, to love him. And this feeling proves to me that I am nothing like the character in your play. I am not, nor have ever been, *Di Bloy Dame.*

49.

Tomasz-Henrik's wife and daughter are in the sunroom. He cradles his wife's face. Devorahleh, he whispers. Then he turns to his daughter and caresses her cheek. Saraleh, he croons.

My heart clamps shut.

His bag waits for him, like a bride, near the piano.

Play for us, Aba, his daughter says. She's in her thirties. Her dark hair loose around her shoulders. It is her best feature. His wife, Devorah, wears a white suit.

Sister Francoise murmurs in my ear—she's a judge in the district court.

Tomasz-Henrik sits at the piano, his back erect. He raises his trembling hands and begins the first notes of the nocturne. Something painful sweeps into the room. Devorah places her hands over his. His face collapses.

Not that one, my love, play something gay.

He takes a deep breath. His fingers pluck out a waltz and I am lost. His daughter puts her head on his shoulder, and his wife fixes the back of his collar. When he reaches the last note, Sara takes up his bag and Devorah follows. On his way out, Tomasz-Henrik stops before me. He kisses my forehead. Rivkaleh, he says, *mayn ketzeleh.*

50.

I call him Asher. A slip of the tongue. I call him Asher. A mistake, the way mothers mix up their children's names. I call him Asher and tell myself there's no harm in it. Only Leon knows and I know. It's our secret and it's such a relief to finally stop pretending this child is anyone else's but mine. At night when he falls asleep beside me, I'm awash in fantasies of leaving the Street of Shoes with him, going to Jerusalem, north to Naharia, or south to Eilat, places where no one will know us. I imagine Katya relishing her freedom. She and Marek could go anywhere, do anything. How many times has she complained that Leon ties her down, tires her out?

He take all my energy, she says. Parasite, she calls him. Little monster, she calls him, and bites his cheek and makes him cry.

I begin to plan, slowly at first, innocuously slipping bits of mine and Leon's clothing into a suitcase just to see how they'd look there, no more than an experiment. My plum skirt next to his khaki shirt with the orange tiger decal.

I call Rothman. How much can I get for the apartment? I say.

Thought you didn't want to sell.

I'm thinking about it.

I imagine him joining us. Driving us up the coast to Naharia, or down through the Arava Desert to Eilat. We'd be a family the way we were always meant to be. Each night while Leon sleeps in my arms, my mind races with plans. Friday morning the suitcase is packed. I cash all of my traveler's checks in the bank. I can barely eat or sit still. The week is done. All I have to do is wait for Katya to bring Asher to me on Sunday afternoon.

It rains all day. My body hurts with waiting and wanting. The ticking clock wears me down. I've arranged for a taxi to take us to Ashdod. From there we'll continue on a bus to Eilat, where I have a reservation under an assumed name at one of the resort hotels on the Red Sea. We'll take a glass-bottom boat. Schools of angelfish will swim in coral cities beneath our feet.

I'm stationed at the balcony window so I can see Katya coming down the street with Leon. At four fifteen I wait outside. By four forty-five, I'm wringing my hands, fighting off a sickening dread. At five, I can barely breathe and dash to Katya's bungalow.

Mila, the young woman from Ukraine, answers the door.

Where's Katya? I peer inside. The television is on too loud, and there are flickering shadows on the wall above the sofa.

They're gone, she says.

What do you mean, gone? To work, the hotel?

They left yesterday night.

Left? Who?

Katya and Leon.

I don't understand. I wrap my arms around my waist, feeling that I must hold myself together, that I am fractured down the middle. My lungs refuse to fill with air. The light is dim so I cannot see Mila's expression.

Marek get job in Haifa docks.

A job?

And apartment. Katya very happy.

That's not possible, I say. Leon is supposed to be with me. They have to be here.

I push past her into the apartment, calling for Leon, only I'm so distraught that I am howling Asher's name. I open the closets in Katya's room. They're empty, not even a hanger left on the rod.

You go home now. Mila takes my hand to lead me out the door.

Leave me alone, I cry, and charge through the apartment, this time searching behind curtains, tearing open cabinets, crawling on my belly to peer under the beds.

I call police, Mila shouts.

I pay no attention to her. All I want is my baby, certain Katya is hiding Asher from me. Before long, strangers are looming over me, asking my name. My body shakes as if with cold. Mila has brought in her neighbors. Big men who try to be gentle and the African women who sell fruit on the street. They click their tongues, take hold of my arms, but I wrestle away from them. Head down, I push my way out into the night. The rain has stopped, leaving behind a dense fog, lifelike and monstrous. I have no recollection of how I get back to the apartment. Time is suspended. Like Asher, I float in the blue ether, trapped. The packed suitcase stands upright in the corner like a pillar of salt, a reminder of a land that's lost to me.

Later, after the neighbor who lives in old Shalom's apartment on the floor below, calls Rothman and tells him he smells smoke, tells him that I refuse to open the door to let him in, Rothman rushes over. He finds me in the living room, cradling Asher's blue-and-green sweater, the suitcase thrown open, the contents in flames. I don't notice that there are burns on my hands or that the divorce papers you served me with are ashes at my feet. Rothman throws a blanket on the fire. A cloud of black smoke billows into the room. The rug I bought for Leon is a circle of scorched earth.

What were you trying to do? he says, but he already knows the answer.

51.

Sister Francoise and I climb the stairs to the fourth floor, to the room of last resort. It's a black box theater, a house for ghosts. I breathe in the greasepaint and chalk dust, the canvas and acrylic blues and reds. Dust motes tremble in the lone spotlight pooling on the stage.

Places. Sister Francoise claps her hands and then retreats into the wings.

I climb onto the bed perched center stage. Dr. S is beside me. His meerschaum pipe with the wolf carving is in the pocket of his sports jacket. He smells of smoked cherries.

How are you today, my dear? How's our boy? he asks.

Sister Francoise emerges with Asher in her arms and places him in mine.

Look who's here, I say to Asher, lifting him up so he can see the matron banging a drum and the camp children holding hands. They circle the bed. Behind them I see Mama in her winter fur, her hands buried in the fox fur muff. Papa is beside her, dressed in his army uniform, the sleeve stained with another man's blood. There is Lenya looking regal in a black felt hat, and Tomasz carrying a fleet of boats made of bark and poplar leaves. I call out for Rothman, and in a moment, he's beside me, dressed in his leather cap and wool pants, wearing the winter coat his sister bought before we left Krosniewice. They greet me and Asher with hugs and kisses. The children—Roza, Micha, Tzila, Wolfe, and Shmulik—clamber up onto the bed to coo at Asher, who rests his head on my breast. He gazes at them with his large almond eyes. All of us talking and laughing. Rothman takes out a flask of vodka.

May I? I turn to Dr. S. Just a *bisel*, a drop, I say.

It's all right if you keep it a small one, he says. This is serious business. He points to a lit apparatus that resembles a large shortwave radio with gauges and wires.

Sister Francoise removes my shoes and socks.

Is that really necessary? I ask.

It'll make things easier, she says, strapping my ankles into the restraints.

Dr. E steps out from behind the curtain, dressed in her white medical coat. She pulls on a pair of latex gloves and nods to Sister Francoise. Rothman tells a joke. The children roll on their backs with laughter. He hands out black market cigarettes.

Lenya removes a lighter from her bag and says, He's certainly learned a thing or two about scrounging.

Rothman gives the signal, and the matron stops banging her drum. The circle parts and the children climb down off the bed and take their places. Mama and Papa smile encouragingly. I turn to the auditorium, and you are there, striding down the aisle.

Lieblings, you say, and wrap your arms around us. Asher smiles and gives you his open-mouthed kiss.

You're here. I caress your cheek and kiss your eyes. I kiss them shut, Max.

Where else would I be? you say.

The houselights dim and the stage lights come up. Chopin's nocturne fills the air. We are cast in shades of blue.

It's time, Dr. E says.

Sister Francoise fills a hypodermic with a golden liquid.

You let go of my hand and cradle Asher in your arms. The circle widens and everyone applauds.

I float up past the battens to the ceiling, beyond the rafters and the rooftop, past the statue of Saint Joseph and the *Collège des Frères*, above the pines, and high above the sea. I climb to where the stars glow and the shattered souls gleam.

Acknowledgements

My deepest gratitude goes to my editor, Joseph Olshan, and publisher, Lori Milken for believing in this novel and shepherding it into the world with such grace. Thank you to Mina Manchester and the entire team at Delphinium Books for their support, and to Colin Dockrill, for his bold and beautiful artistry. Further thanks go to my agent, Murray Weiss.

My study of the theater and acting began decades ago at Tel-Aviv University and continued long after I returned to New York City. I had many wonderful teachers and what I learned in their studios found its way into the heart of this narrator and novel. My immense thanks go to all of them. My Israeli teachers: Nola Chilton, z"l, Rina Yerushalmi, Reuven Adiv, z"l, Benyamin Tzemach, z"l, the formidable dancer and teacher, Rina Shaham, z"l, and the talented and prolific director, Hanan Snir. My American teachers: Herbert Berghof, z"l, Marge Linney, Kay Carney, David Garfield, and the director, Bill Prosser. All of my teachers taught me to listen, to respond, to be authentic, and always search for the truth in my characters, in my life, and in my art. It is everything that I continue to strive for.

Thank you to dear friends Linda Guyette, Julia Hirsch, Rosanne Limoncello, and Louise Marburg for reading early drafts of this book with such care and thoughtfulness.

My heartfelt thanks go to my family: my daughters Shoshi and Becca, their partners, Mari Karppinen and Ian Grunert, and my granddaughters, Alma and Liia who truly light up our lives. To my sister, Esther,

About the Author

Zeeva Bukai is the author of a previous novel, *The Anatomy of Exile.* Her stories have appeared in *Smashing the Tablets: A Radical Retellings of the Hebrew Bible*, CARVE, *Lilith*, *McSweeney's, Quarterly Concern*, *Image Journal*, *December Magazine* and elsewhere. Her honors include fellowships at the Center for Fiction, Hedgebrook, and Byrdcliffe AIR program. She is the Assistant Director of Academic Support at SUNY Empire State University and lives in Brooklyn with her family.